The Rush Cutter's Legacy

Sara Alexi is the author of the Greek Village Series.
She divides her time between England and a small village
in Greece.

http://facebook.com/authorsaraalexi

With thanks to Mary

Sara Alexi

THE RUSH CUTTER'S LEGACY

oneiro

Published by Oneiro Press 2015

This edition 2015

ISBN-13: 978-1519567673

ISBN-10: 1519567677

Also by Sara Alexi

Chapter 1

What must it be like to travel at such a height and at such speed? Can you feel either of those things, or is it like standing still, like you are on the ground and there is no real sense of moving anywhere at all?

Leaning to one side, Vasso can see more clearly through a gap in the vine leaves all the way up to the intense blue sky. Far, far above, a feathering of white froth trails behind a tiny silver plane.

How small it looks – just a sliver of reflected sun. And if they, in their huge aeroplane, look so small from down here, how small the village must look to them. Will they even notice it, these few dozen terracotta roofs, a cluster of whitewashed walls, the grand dome of the church and the central square, reduced to the size of a handkerchief from up there? All around the village are rows and rows of orange trees in their orchards, olive trees dotted in the fields, each farm a patchwork of squares spanning out towards the neighbouring villages, more clusters of terracotta roofs and whitewashed walls, nestling in the plain by the sea, spreading as far as the semicircle of mountains to the north. How inconsequential and small her world must seem to them. They, who will be going off to the islands for a summer of fun, visiting amazing places and staying in luxury hotels, or trailing around the vast ruins and gazing at ancient sites. How amazing the world is for some people these days. It's no wonder so few of them step beyond the designated paths to seek out places like this village, even if it is full of the complexities of real lives. Why would anyone be here when there is so much to see in the world? How many tourists has she ever seen pass by her kiosk in the square? One, maybe two a year: smartly dressed, in new cars, and usually lost, seeking somewhere else, somewhere more mainstream. Always on their way to somewhere else.

If they knew all that went on here, would they want to stay a little longer, explore a little more? If only they knew how much more drama happens for real here. More than is ever produced on the ancient stages at the Herodes Atticus or Epidaurus. They would come in their busloads. Or maybe they would not. Maybe they would still be high up in the sky, heading to more exotic locations!

'Here you are, Vasso.' Juliet puts two glasses of frothy coffee on the table, ice clinking and chiming against the sides. 'What are you looking at?' She peers up through the tangle of vines, following Vasso's gaze.

'Ah, nothing, just a plane.' Vasso takes the glass, its surface slippery with condensation. The day is cooling a little now, and the hills beyond Juliet's whitewashed walls have taken on a pink tinge. The cicadas, relentless in the heat of the day, are calming their rasping love songs. 'You've travelled a lot, Juliet. Tell me, what it is like up there so high, moving so fast? Can you feel it?'

'I don't think going to England and back a few times to see the boys could be considered travelling a lot, Vasso!' Juliet sits back in the hammock that hangs from the pergola over her terrace, her legs stretched out before her, feet bare, nails painted.

Vasso laughs. 'There are people in the village, the old women, for example, who have never been to Athens, much less on a plane! What's it like?' She looks down at her feet, in their worn flip-flops, and notes that her nails need cutting.

'Have you never been on a plane?' Juliet asks, and Vasso tuts a no. 'It's rather cramped, a lot of people in one place. I've been told that longer flights are better as you get more legroom. And a choice of films to watch.'

'Like at a cinema!' Vasso tucks her legs back in against the sofa.

'Yes! Well, no, not exactly. The screen is in the back of the seat in front, so it's more like TV. You must have seen such things in films.'

'Ah yes, now you mention it.' The coffee is sweet and cold. Leaning back in Juliet's sofa, Vasso can see nothing of the hill beyond the wall, but, from behind the house, from beyond Juliet's lovely garden, beyond the nearest orange grove, drifts the sound of goat bells as the animals are herded in for the night. They chime and clang as they do when the animals are hurrying, the dog no doubt at their heels.

'I always had the impression you'd travelled a bit. I don't know why. I guess because you seem to know a little about everything.' Juliet puts her feet up on the arm of the old sofa, using her toes to push back the white throw that mostly covers the worn fabric underneath. She pushes her seat gently back and forth, letting her head rest against the canvas.

'Me, travel!' The thought seems strange, but exciting, and it makes Vasso laugh, which starts Juliet laughing too. This makes Vasso laugh all the more, only she doesn't really know why. Once started, the laughter doesn't stop.

There are those in the village who sometimes treat her as if she is a little simple just because she likes to laugh, and once upon a time she cared what they thought. Now she has reached an age where she is happy to throw reserve to the winds, and she laughs at any little thing she likes. It makes her feel young, defies time's ceaseless march, and pushes back middle age, which in truth has otherwise taken a firm hold.

'The farthest I have been is Orino Island. Well, I went to Athens once, but it doesn't count. It was only for a day.' The words come out between the remains of her chuckles.

'Really?' Juliet seems genuinely surprised. A cat jumps down from the wall and begins a tour of the terrace, sniffing cautiously.

'Really. And I was only meant to be on Orino for a summer, but as it turned out...'

'As what turned out?' Juliet lazily scrapes the froth off the sides of her glass with the straw and then runs the straw through her mouth.

'Ah, you know, life has a way of not going as planned.'

'Now you're intriguing me.' Juliet puts her glass on the floor as the cat jumps onto her knee, back arched in anticipation of strokes, tail up, purring loudly. Juliet scratches the animal under its chin and its paws knead her lap. Soon, it turns round once and collapses into a sleeping heap. Juliet continues to stroke it absent-

7

mindedly. 'Am I sensing one of your stories here, Vasso?'

It's true, she always has a story to tell, but usually someone else's. In the kiosk all day every day, she hears everything. But her time on Orino Island – that is her own story, and feels much harder to tell, if she is to tell it at all.

'You know something, Vasso, we've been having coffee like this quite often for – what, about a couple of years now, since just after I came? I don't mean this unkindly, but you know all about me moving here from England, and the divorce and so on. You know all about my lovely boys and their studies and careers and Thomas's wedding. You know all about my business, and how I make my living. Well, I know how you make your living, too, of course. But what I mean is, I know so very little about you!'

Vasso opens her mouth to speak, but she is not sure what she can say. 'There's not much to tell. I'm just someone, a no one, who grew up in a village. Compared to your life, to anyone's life, there is nothing to tell.'

'You are not a no one! Tell me about Orino Island! I'm sure your life has been just as full as anyone else's.' Juliet stops swinging, her look intense.

'It was just a different time, and I was only sixteen. Thirty-odd years ago! Also the

8

world was different then. People didn't travel so much, so what felt like a long way at the time is just a day's outing now.'

'Tell   me.'   Juliet's   voice   softens, encouraging.

How long has it been since she thought about Orino Island? Years, probably. Years and years. But now, with just this little prompt, a rush of emotion, containing lonely memories of rejection, swamps her.

'Oh, well that's a surprise.' Using her index finger, she wipes away the tears that threaten to fall, and then pats at her perfectly lacquered hair.

'Vasso? Are you crying?' Juliet sits upright, leans forward.

'No, no, no. Well, a bit, yes, it seems so.' She wipes away another tear.

'About going to Orino Island?'

'Well, I was very young. Just turned sixteen, and my mama heard there was a job there that came with a room. She said it wasn't far, a bus ride and then the little taxi boat across and I would be there. We needed the money, you see.'

Chapter 2

It was strange, leaving the village - looking around her and knowing she would not see it again for a couple of months. Things she didn't normally notice or think about took on a special meaning. She looked up at the end window of the school on the edge of the village, which she had stared out of last year, wishing that lessons were finished as the teacher's voice droned and the sunshine called her. Then there had been that delicious moment she walked out on her fifteenth birthday, knowing she need never step through the gates again. Those moments all seemed so close and so real as the bus sped out of the village towards the hills, away from the only place she had ever known as home.

The bus journey was very like the ride into Saros, only longer – much longer. The view from the window was pretty much the same as well, just more of it; row after row of orange trees lining the road, and later olive trees and then scrubland as they climbed up and up, twisting and turning until she felt sick and leant into the aisle to look out of the front window to regain a sense of balance. She tried closing her eyes but that just drew images of the village and all she was leaving.

There were some aspects of it that she would not miss. The strange sort of urgency that her girlfriends seemed to have developed since leaving school, for example, and the boys she had always regarded as friends suddenly becoming tongue-tied or, worse, cocky and arrogant. She understood what it was all about but something told her there was no one in the village for her so it felt… Well, almost as if she did not belong like she once did.

The bus climbed up and up the dusty mountains, leaving the plain and the orange trees behind, and then started a winding descent to the sea on the other side. The bus lurched alarmingly round the bends. Several times Vasso spied the sea in the distance and thought they must be near, but on and on they went until she could stand no more. Finally, the bus swung a hard right and they juddered down an unpaved road, crunching to a dusty halt by a crumbling stone farmhouse. Only she, an old lady and a man with a fine moustache had still to get off and so she followed these adults, past the farm buildings, and down a path to a concrete jetty.

Sitting on the sloping wooden bench on the jetty and looking out to sea, wondering, but not daring to ask, how soon the boat would arrive, Vasso experienced the strangest of sensations. It was a sense of real urgency, a prompting that she needed to be somewhere, but she had no idea where or for what reason. She looked around to find the cause of this sensation but there was nothing to see. It was as if she was meant to meet someone and had forgotten. Was this connected with home? Was there something she had forgotten to do before she left? Try as she might, she could recall nothing she had left undone, and slowly the nagging sensation lifted and was gone.

The old lady sat on the rickety wooden bench next to her and looked across the water. The island, which gave the illusion of being quite close, stretched its fingers into the calm blue sea to the east and west. It looked barren, with no sign of a house, let alone a town. Clutching her bag, which contained her best dress, her Sunday shoes, the letter from Mama's cousin, and a very small handful of drachmas, Vasso could not decide if what she felt now was fear or excitement. Already she missed her mama, but as she had only set out from the village two hours ago she knew this was just a reaction to being so far from home and so she shrugged and looked across the water.

'It will be natural to feel homesick,' Mama had told her as they sat on the doorstep looking up at the stars the night before. 'If you do not, then I must presume I did not do a good job raising you!'

'Mama, I know I'm going to miss you. I miss you just thinking about being away.'

Her mama had put an arm around her then, and pulled her close.

'And I will miss you, my little doll. But the way we must deal with this is to look forward. It is only for a short time – one summer. You will get to know my cousins, and then you and I will be together again.' Vasso had pretended not to notice the moisture in her mama's eyes and the tightening of her grip around her shoulders. She saw wrinkles around the corners of her mama's eyes that she had not noticed before. For a moment the woman next to her was not the mama who had cared for her all her life. She was an old lady, who had worn black since Vasso was a baby. The need for her, at the young age of sixteen, to go and earn a little extra money became not only more understandable in that moment, but a driving necessity.

Her mama sniffed.

'Now, about that tongue of yours, that sometimes gets so tied you cannot speak.' Mama's voice was gentle and kind, but, no matter, her words transported Vasso back to a moment she would rather have forgotten: the school play when she was only eight. She had begged not to be given a speaking part, but her teacher, Kyria Maria, had said it would help her to gain some confidence. Her part was short, just one line, but it was vital for the whole play to make sense. How she had shifted her weight from foot to foot, how she had tried to steady her breathing, twisting her fingers, imagining that the hall was not full of people but was just an empty room into which she must project her voice.

'The room is empty,' she had told herself. 'I will speak the words into an empty room and then the next person will speak and the moment will be forgotten…'

'Vasso, you are on.' Kyria Maria gave her a little push onto the makeshift stage. The empty room suddenly filled as everyone's eyes flicked from Cosmo, the boy narrating, to her, and she could not empty it again. Her palms sweated and she rubbed them together. She spoke the words over and over in her head with her eyes

14

closed, waiting for the moment she must speak, and then there was silence. She opened her eyes to find the whole room looking at her expectantly, and her mouth dried in an instant; her tongue stuck to her palate and her breathing became laboured.

'Go on,' Kyria Maria prompted, and she spoke the first few words of her one line. In a panic, Vasso's voice came out louder than she intended as she completed the sentence. Then her cheeks were on fire and she ran from the stage, through the cluster of parents into the schoolyard, through the gates and home. It took a week and a visit from Kyria Maria before she would return to school.

Her mama continued, bringing her back to the present, 'You must remember that you are just as important as everyone else you ever meet and no one, no matter what they have done or who they are, is better than you.

When Vasso had returned to school, the other children had teased her. Kyria Maria had shouted at them, and that had terrified her. Kyria Maria rarely raised her voice, and this time she, Vasso, had been the indirect cause. It gave her the most uncomfortable feeling of power. It terrified her that she had such power, and her voice became even quieter from that day on. Everything she considered saying she hesitated over, as she worked through in her mind what the consequences could be.

'No better nor worse than you. They are just different.'

How hard her mama tried to give her confidence, and how ashamed she felt that she could not respond and be the daughter she wanted to be.

'We each do what we can in this life.' Her mama patted her hand. 'As for you, you do not know what you will do yet and nor does anyone else, so they are in no position to judge you. So stand tall, you are stronger than you think – just acknowledge the feelings of shyness but do not let them overcome you. And above all, above everything, know you are loved.'

Vasso smoothed down her long hair and sat taller, filling out her chest with air so as not to appear quite so frail. A dot out to sea, near the island, slowly grew in size, gaining shape, until at last the little boat pulled alongside the jetty, bobbing and dipping as the captain skipped on shore to tie her up.

'Orino Island,' he announced, as if there were anywhere else they could be going. The man with the moustache jumped on board, and the old woman slowly stood and shuffled towards the boat. The captain took her wrinkled hand and his biceps bulged, taking the strain, as he helped her on board.

'Orino Island?' he said again, looking straight at Vasso, and she stopped being an observer and became a participant. The boat pitched more than she expected as she stepped off the pier, and she found that she, too, gripped the man's arm quite firmly to descend into the craft.

The vessel was just a fishing boat with an awning for the sun, and they sat around the edge and Vasso held on tight. The old lady kept her hands in her lap and swayed with every movement whilst the man with the moustache struck up a conversation with the captain, about hunting on the mountains of Orino Island in the winter. The motor seemed to have very little power and they made slow progress. The engine was housed in the centre of the boat in a box that reverberated like some giant's musical instrument. This rattling box was also the unsure resting place for a pile of fishing nets, tangled and encrusted with withered seaweed and smelling strongly of fish. Vasso tucked her feet under her and looked in the direction they were travelling. The bow of the boat threw up a foamy wave that threatened constantly to wash over the sides, but never quite did, and after a while Vasso began to relax and enjoy the motion.

As they neared the island it was with some excitement that she recognised that what she had taken to be a tumble of rocks in a cleft in the island was in fact roofs of houses cascading down a very steep slope, right down to the sea. She let out a little gasp at the town's beauty. Undulating burnt-umber tiles, supported on slithers of whitewashed walls, formed steps up the hillside. This cubist pattern was broken up here and there by the rounded dome of a church. A dark-green band of trees crowned the town and, above this, the island was bald, with a rocky grey outcrop, bare, sun-baked and barren.

'Have you not been before?' the old woman asked.

'No, never.'

'Lived there all my life.' The old woman screwed up her eyes and pushed her chin forward as she peered at the island. 'When we get closer you will see the cannons…'

'Cannons?'

'Yes. It was a rich island, you see. Then and now. And so pirates would come. So they put cannons up either side of the port. Can you see them yet?'

Vasso screwed up her eyes like the woman and pushed her chin forward. Could she? Could she see little black dots that might be cannons? Yes, she could!

'I see them!' her excitement filled her words, and for some reason the old lady chuckled.

'Didn't work,' she said, her merriment subsiding.

'What do you mean? The cannons didn't work?'

'No, the idea. By the time the islanders had got to the port and readied the guns, the pirates had usually landed.'

'Oh.' The black spots were clearer now. On one side of the port they were mounted on a high cut-stone wall, and on the other side they sat low, closer to the water's edge.

'So they put a chain. Slung it from one side to the other, but under the water.'

'Under the water?' Vasso turned to watch the woman's face.

'Under the water! It caught the keels of the pirate boats and held them fast while they loaded the cannons and opened fire!'

Vasso caught herself gaping and closed her mouth.

The captain joined in. 'They say the chain is still down there, somewhere. Sunk to the bottom. Too heavy to raise.'

'That's so clever.' Vasso looked back at the island with a sense of awe.

'But you will find we were clever in many ways,' the old lady continued. 'As a newcomer to the island you will find yourself lost again and again. The streets are so narrow, twisting and turning between the buildings, like a maze.'

The idea of being lost did not appeal at all to Vasso and she swallowed heavily and, with a frown, looked back at the town, trying to gauge its size, and wondering just how lost she could get.

The engine cut to a gentle throb and their speed slowed as they trickled into the harbour. As she stepped onto the security of dry land she passed a couple of drachmas to the captain, and the old woman wished her '*sto kalo*'. The man with the moustache raised his cap to her and strode off.

And there it was again – the sensation that she needed to be somewhere, or find someone. It was so strong an urge it sent her turning in circles, looking about her, but it made no sense. Was this just part of missing home, or feeling alone? No, there was no panic to it, no sorrow or sadness. Just an urgency.

Chapter 3

After a while, the feeling eased and her heart stopped pushing against her ribcage. Deep breaths helped her feel more normal and she wiped the perspiration from her brow with the handkerchief Mama had insisted she take with her.

She should find her mama's cousin. What was his name again? With the flat of her hand she smoothed out the tangles that the wind had blown into her hair on the way over, and took out the letter.

Kyrios and Kyria Lakanokoptis, Harbour Side Taverna, she read. If it was on the harbour side, perhaps it was visible from where she was standing. The harbour formed three sides of a square, with a broad, smooth stone walkway between the water and the buildings, shop fronts on the ground floor and balconies above. It was as if the busiest street in Saros had been lifted up and stretched around the water's edge. Above and behind this first row of buildings, the town stretched up the steep hillside, with houses layered upwards – some of them grand, solid square buildings like those on the waterfront in Saros, and others nothing more than whitewashed cottages like those in the village. A real mix, but nothing modern, nothing new, and every roof tiled just as in the old days and all of the shutters painted blue or blue-grey.

On the sea wall, which almost closed the square of the harbour, she found the walkway covered with tables laid with clean white cloths. Beyond these were more tables, which, judging by their bare wooden surfaces, belonged to a café.

On the corner beyond, there was no choice but to make her way past the donkeys lined up there. Mama had warned her about this.

'Now, be aware that there are donkeys,' she had said, and Vasso had winced. 'None of that, now. You are a woman now, not a child to be scared of the donkeys.'

'Yes but…' she had begun.

'There is no choice. There are no roads on Orino, only narrow paths, so everything is hauled by donkeys. Maybe this is a time for you to make your peace with the gentle beasts.'

Nonetheless, Vasso gave the sleepy animals as wide a berth as she could. Looking at them was fine, and she admired their fluffy long ears, their pale muzzles, the black cross over their shoulders, but since being bitten by a neighbour's donkey when she was six she had harboured a fear of the beasts, and would not go near them unless she had to.

'They will not harm you,' said a young man, somewhat older than Vasso, who was loosely holding a rope attached to one of the halters. His hair was a sandy brown, as was his moustache, and there was something about him that felt far away, as if he were not really part of his surroundings.

'Which is Harbour Side Taverna?' Vasso asked, maintaining a steady distance from the animals.

The donkey man looked along the walkway and pointed to the cloth-covered tables. Vasso tried to say thank you, but her fingers interlocked and twisted on themselves and not a sound would come out. So she nodded instead and took quick, short steps towards the taverna.

There were a few people sitting at the tables, each with a drink, and a couple with some food. She should go in and introduce herself. She could hear her own breath quicken. After smoothing the front of her blouse, she stood a little bit taller, lifted her chin up, remembered Mama's love and walked inside.

The place was dark after the glare of the harbour; the walls were stone and the floor tiled. Towards the rear, down one wall was a counter, behind which were various grills and cookers where a tall, thin man was busy. There was only one table inside, up against this counter. Here sat a very large woman, absorbed in a magazine that was laid out next to a full ashtray and an empty coffee cup. Presumably all the other tables and chairs were outside for the summer; the lack of furniture made the place feel hollow, cave-like, almost abandoned.

'Ah, you must be Vasso!' The large woman's chair scraped across the floor as she stood. With a half-smile that did not reach her eyes and her arms limply open, a cigarette firmly remaining between the fingers of her right hand, she waddled forward and loosely embraced Vasso, placing a kiss on each cheek and releasing her quickly. She smelt of tomatoes and oil. 'Argyro,' she introduced herself. From out of the shadows, the tall man, who walked with a stoop, came forward, wiping his hands on a white cloth. 'And this is Stamatis.' Stamatis had the slightest resemblance to her mama – the merriment and kindness of his eyes, and the twist of humour about his mouth. It was enough to increase the aching for home that she had in her chest. She wanted to flee, return home, to have her mama's arms around her.

'Welcome, welcome to you, Vasso.' He smiled kindly as he took her by her hands and studied her face. She could feel the heat in her cheeks and could not meet his eye. 'You are very welcome,' he said gently, and released her hands.

'Come,' Argyro interrupted, 'there is food if you want it, but we will be busy soon so I will show you your room. You can leave your bag there, freshen up, and then, maybe, if you are not too tired you can join us back here. It is quiet at this hour, so a good time for you to start work, I think.' Having said this, she led Vasso through a door at the back of the taverna and out to a small gloomy courtyard that was in need of some care and attention. The only redeeming feature, as far as Vasso could see, was a central, somewhat stunted lemon tree, whose branches were much in need of pruning. The walls, once whitewashed, were now grey, and in one corner a stack of burnt pans was half buried amongst fallen twigs and leaves. There were two doors leading off the courtyard: a solid wooden gate, firmly shut, and a door that stood open to a little room. Inside the room was a single bed, with a pile of slightly grey sheets folded on the end of a sagging mattress. At the end of the bed, through a narrow opening, Vasso could just see the edge of a toilet seat. In the bathroom the paint was peeling and shearing off. Pipes ran exposed along the walls, and the odd weed, both in the courtyard and in the little room, had made a noble effort to grow in a corner or a crevice but had since dried to a crisp in the summer's heat.

'You will be okay here,' Argyro told her. 'There is a shower attachment through there. You make your hair tidy and come back to the taverna.' Left alone, Vasso stood in the courtyard, picturing in her mind Mama's colourful geraniums in pots around the front and back doors, and her own little bed with a cover her yiayia had made with bobbins and yarn on her twisted fingers the year before she was gone.

Vasso crossed herself three times in memory of Yiayia and then, trying to walk right over the fluttering feelings that threatened to twist her throat speechless and knot her stomach into spasms, stepped into the room, put her bag down, twisted her hair over her shoulder and quickly and neatly made up the bed, smoothing the sheets with the flat of her hand. She washed her face in the cracked sink by the toilet and then combed her hair, plaited it into one long tail and, feeling neater, strode back to the taverna.

'Everything alright?' Stamatis asked, a frown passing across his lifted brow.

'Ah, there you are.' Argyro smiled broadly and, taking Vasso by her arm, her big hands closing all the way around it, led the way to the taverna's entrance.

'So, just stand here,' she said, placing Vasso just inside the door, facing outwards. 'Watch Spiros.' Argyro pointed at a young man in black trousers, black waistcoat and a white shirt, who had his back to them. 'Today just learn from what you see him do, and if anyone looks like they need anything and Spiros is inside, you go and serve them.'

Then she was left alone.

There were twelve tables, each seating four people. If they were all in use, how could she keep an eye on them all? She could take two plates at a time but she just didn't have the strength to line them up her arm as she had seen waiters do in Saros town. For now, only three tables were occupied, but if it were to get any busier, what then?

As she pondered this possibility the man in the waistcoat turned round and, catching her looking at him, smiled broadly.

Vasso stepped back, steadied herself with her hands on the wall. Her earlier sensation of urgency had returned and knocked her off balance. It was him! This stranger standing

27

before her, this young man she had never seen before in her life, eclipsed everything. The sensation left her reeling and her emotions overwhelmed her. Looking at the ground, she tried to block him out of her mind, regain her control.

Taking her palms from the wall, she noticed that her hands were shaking. She intertwined her fingers in front of her but it helped very little.

He finished what he was saying to a customer, and, turning around, came towards her. He would not notice her. People seldom did. He would probably, if he did anything, give her a curt nod and walk straight past.

Here he came.

She must breathe. She had forgotten to breathe.

So close now. If she stood still he would have to brush past her, but her feet were stuck. Her limbs would not respond. '*Den eimaste kala*,' she whispered to herself.

'You must be Vasso.' He was standing so close, looking right into her eyes. He noticed her! *Panayia*, she had been noticed! Now he was waiting for her to answer. What could she say? What should she say? Her lips were parted but no words seemed to come.

'Stars in the heavens, you are beautiful,' he said.

The directionless, inexplicable yearnings, the churning sensation, the sense of urgency were now all explained, and clear, and focused. This stranger she had never seen before was the cause of it all, without a doubt!

And her legs gave way and the world became black.

Chapter 4

'Put a damp cloth on her head.'

'No, give her air. Carry her outside.'

'Move back, come on. Just give the poor girl some room.'

'Vasso, Vasso, are you alright?'

The world swam as if through water that had been poured on glass, and everything sounded unfamiliar. Where was Mama's voice?

'I still say put a damp cloth on her head.'

'Well, get one, then.' This voice sounded annoyed.

Blue. It must be the sky, and the dark outline of a head, fuzzy at the edges.

'Lift her up a bit.'

'No, keep her head down so the blood flows.'

'Vasso, can you hear me?'

Too low a voice to be her mama's, but maybe she just wasn't hearing clearly.

'Mama?'

'No, Spiros. You fainted.'

The man with the smile who said... No! She must have been dreaming.

Focus came to the things nearest her first, and one of these was Spiro's face. Such a kind face – such a generous smile.

'Ahh, there you are,' he said.

'Here, I have a cold cloth.'

'No, get some water.'

'You okay? Do you want to sit up a little? Here, let me help you,' Spiros said.

And, then, such a firm arm around her, lifting her as if she were a feather.

'Do you want a sip of water? Let me help.' His arm was still supporting her.

The cold against her lips felt nice. A small sip and the icy liquid flowed down her throat, bringing life to her, waking her. Then the flow of heat in her cheeks, and she put a hand on them to hide their colour. How could she faint! On her first day, in her first hour. What would they think of her?

The faces of Argyro and Stamatis took shape, and, with a wriggle, she tried to stand.

'Whoa, steady... Where are you going?' Spiro's firm hands held her down. 'Kyria Argyro, why don't you get a little glass of wine to revive Despinis Vasso?'

'Oh, yes, or brandy. No – wine, you're right.'

'I'll get a cushion,' Stamatis said, and he hurried inside.

'Oh, yes, of course.'

Now there was only Spiros close by, and a pleasant musty smell that had a sweetness to it – a complex perfume.

'You are still beautiful, even after a faint.' He chuckled.

Maybe it was his way of joking, or maybe he liked to tease the girls. Either way, Vasso found herself making a decision to give his words no weight.

A cushion was propped behind her head and a glass was put to her lips. The liquid was red and she expected it to taste sweet, fruity, but it was sharp, like vinegar. She did her best not to spit it out. Mama would not be pleased. The tales she had heard of her own baba and the years Mama had spent in black had been too many. She tried to push away the glass along with the thoughts.

'It's only a little wine,' Spiros implored.

'No, thank you.' By now Vasso was sufficiently recovered to look around and satisfy herself that not too many people were watching. It would be better if she stood now, if people

32

went back to what they were doing. Running a hand over her forehead to push back any stray hairs, she prepared herself to take her own weight and get up on her feet.

'Come, let me help you.' His arm around her tightened and lifted.

'I'm fine, thank you.' She pushed him off and for just a second what looked like fear or hurt passed over his face.

'Okay. So, Vasso, you come sit here. Spiro, there are people who have just sat down at the tables by the water. Stamati, I think I can smell something burning. So, is this a one-off or are you a fainter?' Not only did the words sound hard but there was an edge to her voice, a rasping sound as if she were chewing gravel as she talked. Gone was the broad smile.

'No, I am not a fainter. I mean, I have fainted before.'

'You are too thin. That's what it will be. A puff of wind could take you away. When did you last eat?'

'Well, I had a piece of bread for breakfast, I think.' But in truth she may not have. It had all been a bit of a rush at the last minute, with the bus coming early and people calling round to wish her well before she went.

'Stamatis!' The volume of the woman's screech shocked Vasso almost as much as the fact that one person would ever address another in such a manner.

'Yes, beloved?' He came hurrying from the kitchen area.

'No, stay there. I just need you to bring this girl a plate of something. If you bring *spanakopita* and some chips, you can do me one, too. What time is it? Yes, well, I was up early. Well, don't just stand there.' She turned to Vasso and rolled her eyes. 'Men, eh?' she asked, but obviously expected no reply.

The time it took for the plates of food to be put before them seemed very drawn out and Vasso could think of nothing to say to the woman. Nor did Argyro speak. Instead, she took a toothpick from the dispenser on the table and satisfied herself with picking her teeth and sucking noisily.

'What took so long?' she said as the food was set before them. Stamatis said nothing but hurried back inside and returned with a basket of bread.

Argyro wasted no time in tucking into the food and, once chewing, she seemed to retreat into a world of her own. Vasso nibbled at the *spanokopita*, which was overly salted and decidedly soggy. The chips, on the other hand, were undercooked: crisp and golden on the outside but raw in the centre. She took a drink of water but the glass smelt unclean, as if the washing-up water had been dirty, or the cloth used to dry it had needed a wash.

'You not eating any more?' Argyro asked.

'No, thank you. I feel full.'

'You're a bird! At least you won't cost us in food.' And she stabbed the remainder of Vasso's pie with her fork. 'You can go and wash that and whatever else is in the sink,' she said, nodding at Vasso's plate.

Chapter 5

The state of the sink was perhaps the second shock of the day, after the fainting. Judging by the hour of the day and the few customers outside, what was there must have been left in the sink the night before, but nothing had been soaked and the food was now dried on hard and several flies were buzzing around. As the sink was along the back wall, she opened the door to the courtyard to let a little light in and a few of the flies out.

'You might want to pour some water over all that and leave it to soak before you tackle it,' Stamatis called over to her, but Vasso decided she was here to earn a wage and set to at the sink with quiet energy. It took her the rest of the morning, and when she had finished with the pots she cleaned all around the sink until the place look new, or at least somewhat newer. The improvement was very satisfying and she was glad to be hidden away from public scrutiny.

With the washing-up done, Vasso looked about her for more jobs that needed doing and was surprised when Argyro and Stamatis called out a cheerful *'Adio!'* and left. The clock confirmed that it was two o'clock – about the normal time for a *mesimeri* sleep in the heat of the day, but for a seafront taverna it seemed like a short route to failure. Such places could not afford to close; they must stay open day and night to pull in as much trade as they could, especially in the summer months. She knew, she had seen it. Every Saturday for as long as she could remember she would accompany her mama on the bus into Saros town to buy the week's vegetables at the *laiki*. More often than not, as a little treat, they would go to the harbour front and order a drink, usually just one Greek coffee – the cheapest thing on the menu – and they would sit there watching the tourists walk by, the yachts pulling into the harbour, and for an hour or so feel a part of the bigger world. But how many times had she seen those places on the front open and close over the years? Each new and excited owner thinking that they could earn the rent more easily than the last, only to find themselves closing their doors six months later.

She watched the round figure of Argyro and tall, thin, stooped Stamatis wander along the front and then turn up a narrow lane into the town, and she wondered if coming here had been a good decision. Surely if she had tried she could have found work in Saros? But then what chance had she been given to do that? Mama had offered it as a completed deal, had made all the decisions and arrangements, and it was not as though there had really been a choice.

'They are family, Vasso. At least with family we know you will be treated fairly and you will be safe. Besides, they need someone, so it helps us both,' Mama had said.

'Come on, don't just stand there.' Spiro's words startled her, and then he offered her the smile that made her heart race and with it came the assured feeling that she was definitely in the right place. He swept past her into the taverna and marched behind the counter at the back. So now he was the cook, which presumably made her the waiter. She looked out, expecting to see one or two people and the rest of the tables mostly empty.

But, from nowhere it seemed, quite a few of the tables were now occupied and more people sat down as she watched. She looked to see if a ferry boat had pulled in, finding no other way to account for the sudden business.

'So!' A young man strode in, slapping his hands together and rubbing them. 'What is it today, Spiro?' He sucked in his lips and let them out noisily.

'Today it is *barbounia*. Ilias had a good catch so there will be enough for everyone.' Spiro's face glowed as if he was lit up from inside. His eyes danced and shone and what was already a beautiful face to Vasso became something that could only belong to an angel.

'Ah, and who is this?' The man turned to Vasso, still rubbing his hands together. 'So, you have got yourself some help. That should make things easier. Save us all running backward and forward,' and he laughed.

'This is Vasso.'

'And have you told Vasso your little game?'

'Actually Dimitri, there has not been a moment. But perhaps while I am getting things going you could do the honours.'

'Oh my goodness, that is such pressure on me. If I put it the wrong way and she decides to tell them, we are all sunk.'

'You are very kind, but the truth is only I would be sunk.' A darkness passed over Spiro's eyes and a look of sadness swept over his face that made Vasso decide that, whatever they were talking about, she would tell no one.

Dimitri appeared older than her, but not by much. He, too, had a kind face but his eyebrows were bushy and met in the middle and gave him an edge of severity that caused her to shrink from him a little.

'So, my little mouse,' he addressed her with kindness. 'Will you keep our secret?' As he said this he looked to the door and Vasso followed his lead. With a sharp intake of breath, she saw the tables were now all full. There were women in black, fishermen with their traditional caps, shopkeepers keeping one eye on their shop fronts. There was hardly a seat left empty and the tourists who had sat down before Stamatis and Argyro left were now looking around nervously.

What on earth was going on? Why the sudden rush of customers, and all Greek? It wasn't as if a ship had just docked.

'What...?' was the only word she managed to tease past her lips.

'Now, it is important that you understand everything.' He moved slightly closer to her. 'You see our friend Spiros there?' She nodded. 'Well, he is blessed and he is cursed.'

He didn't look cursed at that moment. He looked happy, pouring oil, sprinkling seasoning, occasional flames licking up, visible above the counter.

'Tell me.' Vasso wanted to know. She wanted to know everything about him.

Chapter 6

'Like I said, blessed and cursed. The curse you know.'

'Do I?'

'Of course you do. Some may not be so unkind as to use the word curse, but my allegiance is to Spiros, and to have those two as parents could be described as nothing else.'

'His parents...?' Vasso was looking out at the tables, the sun shining down on the white cloths, the blue sea behind and everyone looking happy and relaxed, as if they were on holiday. Vasso had to remind herself that she, at least, was not on holiday. Everyone would need serving: the orders taken, written down and delivered, not misremembered. The small piece of *spanakopita* churned in her stomach. She would have to speak to them all.

'Stamatis and Argyro are his parents!' Dimitri exploded, as if she was teasing him, making him spell it out.

'No!' She had not seen that coming. That huge, rough and unpleasant barrel of a woman his mama! Poor Spiros. And he the son of Stamatis? That would mean she and Spiros were related – perhaps third cousins, with great-great-grandparents in common... Working out relatives was very confusing, she concluded.

'Don't look so shocked. Stamatis is a good, kind old man, just a little – how shall I put it – hen-pecked.'

But she could not wipe the emotion from her face and Dimitri started chuckling.

'Argyro has not always been so bad, but it is worse since Spiros came back to the island.' They both turned to watch Spiros, who was now in full flow, shifting back and forth behind the counter and beginning to fill the room with the most amazing smells.

'Come on, the smells are killing us!' someone shouted from outside. Vasso wondered if she should take them out bread, knives and forks, take their orders.

'Dimitri, I have to serve.' But his hand on her arm stopped her from moving.

'You need do nothing. When the food is ready then you take it out.'

'But I need to know what each wants to order.'

43

Dimitri's head rolled back, now, as he laughed, his agile frame shuddering with the movement. 'No,' he managed to say, but he could not stop laughing and wagged a finger to accentuate the 'no' until he caught his breath enough to say it again. 'No!' Finally he regained control. 'No, no orders. They want whatever he cooks.'

Vasso frowned.

'Ah, you see, that's his blessing. He can fry *barbounia* and make them into a dish fit for a king. He can take cabbage and work his magic so it is to die for. He is an alchemist, and you will hear no orders or complaints from out there.' With a jerk of his thumb he indicated the crowd outside. 'We are just glad he has come back to us and we hope he won't go again. But in a moment, if you want, you can take out water and forks, take out some wine, see who wants beers. Until now they have been obliged to serve themselves.'

'So what you are saying to me is that these people have waited until Stamatis left…'

'Exactly.'

'So why doesn't he cook all the time?'

'Yes, indeed, why doesn't he cook all the time? What sort of woman would stop her son cooking if he had skills such as Spiros?' He chuckled as he talked.

'No, I'm serious, why doesn't he?'

'First plate's ready,' Spiros called, and Dimitri nudged her.

'Who is it for?'

'Anyone, everyone!' Spiros passed two plates over the counter to her, his face alive, his movements energised.

Nervously, she took the plates outside and then paused, wondering who to serve first.

'Me.' A man put his hand up. 'I have left a man half-shaved in my chair. Those around him laughed, and Vasso slipped between tables and chairs and set one plate down in front of the barber, and one in front of the man next to him.

'What is it today?' someone asked.

'*Barbounia* like you have never eaten,' said the barber, leaning over his plate and taking a deep breath before picking up his knife and fork.

Vasso returned inside.

'Here you go, Vasso.' Spiros seemed to be vibrating with energy, but when he passed her the plate he did not let it go until she looked him in the eyes, and then with a wink he was back to his pans.

The next hour passed too quickly. After serving the barber, Vasso brought plates for the man who owned the jewellery shop and the woman who served in the bakery, who said she

45

had left a queue of people waiting for the next batch of bread to come out of the oven.

'It needed another fifteen to twenty minutes,' she explained. 'But I will let it burn before I miss this meal!'

They all spoke to Vasso as if she had grown up amongst them, and she began to relax. A group of six men had pulled two tables together, and the stench of fish clung to them.

'Was this your catch, Ilias?' one asked another. They acknowledged Vasso with a nod of the head as she put the fish before them.

'I caught the fish,' came the reply, 'but I swear the mermaids themselves must have had a hand in making them taste so good.' The comment was met with chuckles from several tables around them as eager faces waited their turn.

'Am I too late?' The priest in his long black robe and tall *kalimavkion* hat approached as fast as his waddle would bring him, then pulled a chair up to sit with the only man in a suit. 'Did you close the bank, Gerasimo?' he asked as he sat down.

'For sure! What, you think the need of a loan or the release of a few drachmas is more important than this?' He grinned broadly at his joke, which was received with nods and giggles from tables around him.

The well-meaning banter continued to bounce from one table to another as the food was served, and soon Vasso knew that Gerasimos had been bank manager for over twenty years, and that the Kaloyannis brothers at the next table managed the boatyard along the coast, and were in town to pick up some tools they had ordered from the mainland. The priest made her laugh and put her at ease, and soon she forgot her shyness.

Everyone outside was animated and talkative whilst they waited, silent as they ate and then reflective when they pushed their chairs back and spread fingers over expanded stomachs.

Finally, everyone had been served and Vasso slowed her pace.

'Last two plates,' Spiros said.

'They are all fed.' Vasso replied.

'Just as well.' He looked past her, 'Dimitri!' he called to his friend, holding up the plates before setting them on the counter. With the cooking all finished, Spiros came from behind the counter and, using his forearm, and emitting a huff of disgust, he swept Argyro's magazine off the table onto the floor and sat down heavily, clearly exhausted. Vasso picked the magazine up and found a place for it on the counter and then served him and Dimitri with the two remaining plates.

'Come.' Spiros pulled an extra chair up beside him so both Vasso and Dimitri could sit, and he pushed his plate towards her. The fish was unlike anything she had tasted. The sauce was subtly flavoured, with hints of lemon and basil. She would not have thought her palette was educated enough to appreciate it, and yet each forkful exposed another stratum of tastes. The fish itself was tender and fragrant, with the warmth of the sun and the freshness of the sea offset by the dense richness of sundried tomatoes mixed with the sweetness of garlic. It was an experience unlike any she had had before, nor was it one that she would have deemed possible. She found herself feeling guilty as she made comparisons between this assault on the senses and her mother's cooking, which, although nourishing and healthy, she could now see was unimaginative, to say the least.

'Are you not eating?' Dimitri pushed his plate at Spiros and Vasso did the same, and he ate a little from one and then from the other.

'That was great.' The barber came in and dropped a note on the table, tapped his temple with two fingers and pointed them at Spiros. 'See you tomorrow.' And he left with an ambling gait, a man well satisfied.

'Thanks, Spiro.' A woman with long eyelashes and hands bedecked with jewellery dropped a note of a larger denomination on the table. 'For me and Maria,' she informed him.

And so it continued: the people coming in, leaving some money and wishing Spiros well as he ate, and promising to be back tomorrow. The chairs outside emptied until only the tourist couple remained with their frappes, looking even more confused than before.

Dimitri picked up the money, shuffled it into a pile and handed it to Spiros, who counted the money and sighed.

'Every day you are a little closer to having enough for your own taverna!' Dimitri said.

'It seems such long way off,' Spiros replied, and peeled off a few notes and handed them back.

'Can you give this to Ilias for the fish?'

'Sure. Are you doing fish again tomorrow?'

'I've been talking to the butcher, so maybe not.'

'Are you going to try and catch some sleep, now Vasso is here?' Dimitri did not look at her as he said this, and for the first time she felt an outsider to the adventure that had just taken place.

49

'What, and leave you and her to have all the fun?' he joked, but he looked tired.

'I can clear up.' Her voice came out small, but she felt grateful to be included again by Spiro's words.

'Come on guys, if we all work together we can get it done in time for everyone to catch a nap.' And with new energy he jumped up and headed behind the counter, piling up pans and putting away spices. Vasso followed Dimitri outside and the tables were soon cleared. Dimitri was strong and carried great stacks of plates, whereas Vasso could manage only a few at a time. Not for the first time in her life she cursed her fragile frame.

Vasso washed the pots; they quickly dried in the summer's heat and Dimitri put them away.

'There, I think I have earned my fish. How are you doing, my friend?' Dimitri addressed Spiros.

'Done.' Spiros pulled off his apron and put his waistcoat back on, and looked around at the taverna, which showed no sign of what had just taken place.

'I think I might just grab a few minutes,' he said with a yawn, his hand on his friend's shoulder.

'Sleep well, my friend,' Dimitri said and wandered out into the sunshine.

Vasso continued her work until it was all finished, and it was only when she put the last pan to drain and turned around that she saw Spiros was neither outside nor in. After a moment of panic that it had all been left to her she caught sight of his foot, through the back door, past the lemon tree, hanging off the end of her bed. A gentle snoring sound filtered back to her. With relief, Vasso told herself that if she really needed to she could wake him enough to ask for help.

'Not a customer in sight.' Stamati's voice made her jump.

'Where's Spiros?' Argyro demanded, the two of them blocking the sunshine as they stood in the doorway.

Chapter 7

Vasso opened her mouth, but no words came out. She searched the woman's full face for traces of Spiros but could find none.

'What are you staring at? You're not a starer, are you? I cannot abide people who stare,' Argyro huffed, and folded her arms, looking away. 'Ah, there he is.' She peered through to Vasso's little room. 'Spiro, hey Spiro,' she called, then looked back through the taverna to the tables outside where a family were seating themselves. The man, dressed in white shorts and a brightly coloured T-shirt held out a chair for his wife, who had on a lemon-yellow dress and sun burnt shoulders. The children, both wearing hats and with equally red shoulders, whined and fidgeted. 'We have customers,' bellowed Argyro, and the tourists looked up and seemed suddenly hesitant.

'I'll go,' Vasso offered, and trotted outside, happy to give Spiros a few more minutes' sleep.

The afternoon was relaxed and, after the rush at lunchtime, Vasso found she could take it all in her stride. Spiros slept for only an hour but by ten o'clock that evening Vasso found she was yawning and wished that she, too, had somehow managed to lie down for a moment in the afternoon.

Later still, at around eleven, there was a little burst of foreign diners, but after that the place was empty. Loitering by the doorway, she saw plenty of Greeks dressed up and promenading along the front and then turning up the narrow paths into the town, presumably to eat elsewhere.

'They don't come here.' Argyro stood beside her. 'They are jealous of us, of our harbour front taverna, so they go somewhere else.' She stood, arms folded, filling the doorway. Most people hurried by. Vasso said nothing.

'So, I will go now. Spiros will show you how to close up.' And she went back inside, took her cigarettes off the table, and spoke rapidly to Stamatis. Stamatis hurriedly took off his apron and the two of them went out into the relative cool of the night. As they started to leave, Argyro stopped and had a brief, quiet word with Spiros and pointed in Vasso's direction. Vasso felt the heat rise in her cheeks and she went inside to tackle the last of the pans that Stamatis had burnt that evening.

'They're gone.' Spiros came in with the menus. He went out again with a tray and returned with the salt and pepper pots, the napkin holders and the pots of toothpicks.

'You fancy an ouzo?' he asked.

'Oh, no, thank you.'

'Do you drink at all?'

'No.' That was what she had always said when offered a drink. It was what her mama wanted her to say, and until now she had thought nothing of it. However, just in that second, there was a moment of curiosity. Might she in fact like it? Added to this, she considered that she could choose to be different, here among people whom she did not know and who did not know her.

Spiros went back outside and took off the clips that held the tablecloths in place and, like a matador, whipped off each cloth in turn. The awning that shaded the tables during the day had been gathered in and now the sky was dark and filled with hundreds and thousands of twinkling stars. Spiro's face was highlighted by the moon. She turned back to the sink and made an effort to concentrate, to get the job finished.

The last pan was burnt black inside and out, and she scrubbed it, but to no avail.

'Oh, leave it to soak.' Spiros came in from the little courtyard, which surprised her as she hadn't seen him go out there. 'Come.' He held out his hand towards her. Vasso looked down at her own soapy, water-wrinkled hands and swilled them under the tap, but by the time she had dried them Spiro's own hand was no longer on offer. He was standing by the door to the courtyard with an eager expression on his face.

What on earth was he expecting, she wondered? Could he possibly think that, given a bit of charm and a smile, she would fall willingly into his bed? What kind of man was he?

'Come,' he said again, and Vasso was horrified to find she wanted to obey him.

She stood rigidly. She was not going to give in to such desires. Mama would disown her! It was against all she had been brought up to believe.

'Please, I want you to see what I have done,' Spiros implored.

She took one tentative step towards the door and, on catching sight of a change in the courtyard, she proceeded with more assurance.

'Oh, Spiro!' she gasped.

A few of the lower branches had been sawn off the lemon tree, making room to walk easily under it. The floor had been swept, the

55

pans and leaves had gone from the corner, and two chairs, one of which she recognised from her room, and another from the taverna, had been placed under the moonlit leaves. The side door was open and in the street beyond she could see the lemon tree branches and the pots piled up along with bags of rubbish. Spiros hurriedly closed the door to hide the mess.

But the nicest touch of all, as far as Vasso was concerned, was a candle in a bottle, flickering on the small table he had squeezed between the chairs under the lemon tree.

'I told Argyro that, really, she should have offered you a room at the house,' Spiros grumbled, the words sounding like an apology. 'Stamatis agreed.'

'This is so pretty,' Vasso murmured.

'I will get drinks.' There was relief in his voice now. 'Are you sure you won't have an ouzo with me?'

'No, thank you.' Pleasing him felt amazing, as if she had a great power. It filled her with a sense of importance that she felt sure must show on the outside. Everything around her seemed to glow with colour and the jasmine in the air was almost strong enough to make her dizzy. Even her body felt alive, as if her blood was tingling the inside of her flesh. With his hands on the back of one of the chairs he invited her to sit. Then he went back inside and she could hear a chinking of bottles.

'It's just fruit juice,' he said, putting a drink in front her. His ouzo grew opaque as it mixed with the melting ice in his glass. She sipped with quick glances, trying to form her question before she spoke.

'May I ask you something?'

'Sure.' He seemed so at ease, stretching his arms to the stars, his chest barrelling outwards.

'Why don't they let you cook?'

'Ah.' His hands fell and his chest sank. 'It's a bit of a long story.'

'Oh, alright.' Vasso tried to stop herself staring. His profile in the moonlight was just as perfect as his face in the sun.

'I don't mind telling you, if you want?'

'Tell me.' If he talked she had a reason to keep looking at him.

'Well, I grew up in this taverna. I learned to crawl on that floor.' He pointed through the door to the flagged floor of the taverna, which looked like it needed a good scrub. I learned to walk clutching at the table edges outside, from one to the other. I got so much attention from the customers.'

Vasso could imagine him as a child. The dark, fine hairs down the back of his neck, the long eyelashes edging his eyes in black, his nose probably smaller then but still with the slightly turned-up end. He would have been adorable.

'As I grew, I wanted to be like my mama.'

'Who? Argyro!' The words rushed out with force. Spiro's eyes flashed as they glanced across at her, and he let out a snort and then nodded his head slowly as if he understood the emotion behind her words. The nod became a shake.

'No, not Argyro, she is not my mama. Baba remarried after...'

'Ahhh.' Vasso drew the sound out as she readjusted her thinking. It all made a lot more sense now, even though she did not have the details.

'My mama was the cook. My baba, Stamatis, he was the waiter and I washed up after school. We made a fine business here.' His eyes were unfocused and Vasso presumed he was far away in his memories.

She waited, and after a minute or two he broke his reverie and took a sip of his ouzo before continuing.

'They did well and I helped cook at weekends, learnt a little from my mama. But life is always unpredictable. Not long after I left school, Mama was dead, and then, only a short time later, Argyro was my stepmother.'

'Oh, I am sorry.' It seemed impossible to think what her own world would be like without her mama. Even then, in that very moment, it gave her such comfort to know her mama was at home waiting for her.

'After Mama died I offered to cook. Well, I didn't offer, I just expected that I would be the cook. It was logical. But Argyro was there by my baba's side before Mama was even in her grave. It was she who convinced him that he should be the cook and for some reason he agreed with her. It was as if she had a hold over him. He did whatever she said. It wasn't long before the business stopped doing so well, and we were – are – getting poorer and poorer.'

'Oh dear.' Vasso was not sure what else to say.

Spiros knocked back the last of his ouzo and slammed the glass onto the little three-legged metal table. 'Stamatis – Baba – is a great waiter. The customers love him, he has a good memory for the orders and he is a kind man. But if I was the cook and he was the waiter, what difference would that make to her? There is no reason, no logic.'

'Ahh.' Vasso could see his point.

'So I did as my baba asked, and I became the waiter. She did the washing-up for a while. Until the ring was on her finger, anyway. Then she sat and drank coffee and smoked. The pots piled up in the sink until someone was forced to do something with them, but it was seldom her. It was usually me.'

'But...' Vasso began, but was grateful that her voice was very small as she had no idea what to say, how to sympathise. His words, if anything, made her feel angry.

Then a new thought occurred to her.

'But if you were not allowed to cook, how did you get to be so good at it?'

Chapter 8

There was that sad look again, and every fibre of her wanted to reach out and make his world better, like when Mama was sick, but much more, so much more.

'You seem pained at the thought.'

'She's a dominant woman.' He stated this calmly.

Without a word, he slid from his chair and walked with a heavy step back into the taverna. A cork popped inside and he returned with the glass already to his lips.

'That won't help,' she said, but so quietly he didn't hear her; or maybe he decided to ignore her. After a minute's silence she wondered if he had forgotten her question, or decided not to talk after all. She searched for the best way to ask again, kindly, gently. But she had no need.

'One day she just pushed too far. She humiliated Baba in front of his friends and customers. I tried to intervene but he hushed me, told me I didn't understand everything, that I should not be so harsh on her.'

'"Son," he said, "it's better this way.""What way?" I said. "Her telling us both what to do, you hating every day behind the grill, me wasting my time serving?"'

Spiros fell silent and looked into his glass but he did not drink. There was moisture on his bottom lashes.

'So I waited until everyone had gone and I faced her.' He looked up and into Vasso's eyes, looking for something there, but she could not tell what it was he sought – affirmation? Connection? Approval? Sympathy?

'What happened?' She needed to know.

'She was vicious,' he said. He sounded defeated and the way his shoulders rolled over reminded her of how Stamatis walked, with the same stoop, the same defeat. 'She told me I knew nothing about cooking, that if anyone had ever told me I was good at it they were probably being kind, taking pity on me because my mama had just died. That caught me off guard and I fell into the place of sadness that I feel when I think of Mama. Then she said that, from what she had eaten of my food, it was the worst she had ever tasted.' He drank now and then continued. 'I told her she didn't know what she was talking about. I was shouting at this stage and I said that my mama had taught me and my grandfather had taught her and then she went quiet and this look of horror twisted her face…'

But Vasso did not care about Argyro. She cared about Spiros and right then she wanted to reach out and put her hand on his arm, to show him she believed in him. But she faltered. To actually touch him would be too much, it was not right. Spiros was oblivious, however, and he continued his recollection.

'"Stop!" my baba shouted, and he rushed over to be by her side. "Ah, I see", Argyro said quietly then. "So you bring your grandfather into this, do you? Now I understand." Or something like that. Anyway, that was all she said and my baba's arms were around her and he looked at me as if I had committed the worst crime on earth whilst she wept into his shoulder. Well, she made the noises, anyway, but when she lifted her head his shirt seemed dry.

'But I was mortified at the look he gave me. I felt abandoned. "Baba, tell her I can cook!" I demanded. But my baba did not answer me so I stormed out of the taverna.' Spiros glanced at Vasso, who became conscious that her mouth had dropped open. 'This was only two years ago, but I was a lot younger then. My temper was shorter and my ego was larger.' He took a mouthful of ouzo, swilling it around his cheeks.

'What happened when you went back?'

'Ah, well, that was the thing. I didn't go back, not until three weeks ago.'

'Three weeks?' At this, Vasso readjusted her perceptions. She had presumed she was walking into a steady business. Actually, steady wasn't quite the right word. When Argyro was there the place felt tired, as if no energy had been injected into it for years. But then there was the lunchtime service. How had the whole lunchtime event become so well established – so seamless – so quickly? Had it been orchestrated or had it just happened? She was about to ask when a further thought caused a frown to rimple her brow. If things had changed so dramatically quite recently then there was also the potential for them to change quite dramatically again in the future. Like Dimitri said, it would only be a matter of time before Argyro and Stamatis found out about the lunchtime service, and then what? Might she lose her job because she had been party to it all? Or would Spiros have to go? If that happened could she stay – and would she want to stay?

Also, her mama had arranged her appointment here more than three weeks ago – presumably before Spiros had returned to the island. Now that he was back, was she still really wanted or was she being kept on out of politeness, or, worse, out of pity? Why had they not informed Mama that their son had returned, and that she wasn't needed?

It all suddenly seemed so very complicated. If she were to take the initiative, and bring up the subject herself, would that be a positive thing? Or might it give Stamatis and Argyro the opportunity to tell her she was not needed? Perhaps it would be better to leave it all up to Mama and Stamatis. Then again, surely at sixteen she should have some input into her own life? One thing was sure – putting distance between her and Spiros was the last thing she desired.

'When I walked out I had some money on me.' He patted his breast pocket, where the drachmas from lunchtime bulged. 'So I caught the last boat across to the mainland. I had nowhere to go so the first night I just slept on the jetty, looking back over here, trying to get a better perspective on everything.'

As Vasso watched him talk he seemed to become more and more lost to the outside world. His words filled her own head with the images, and she could see – and feel – the story he told.

Chapter 9

The island hadn't seemed such a great distance away. When he was younger, he and his friends had once or twice dared each other to swim across, but they very seldom went further than the last of the fishing boat buoys. It had seemed such a long way, back then. Now he was actually on the mainland it did not feel far enough. What had possessed Baba to marry such a woman? Sure, he was sad about Mama, they both were, but that didn't excuse – or explain – him running out to marry the first person that came along.

But, to be fair to his baba, had he actually had a choice? For days, he had wandered from room to room, down to the port and back, looking like all the muscles had been removed from his face. He had hardly spoken a word for weeks, and every morning Spiros emerged from under his own sheet of gloom to check that his baba had lived through the night, that he had not gone and thrown himself off the coastal path into the sea or taken the bread knife to his veins. Had he even had a chance to emerge from this deep state of mourning to make a clear-headed decision about anything, let alone marriage?

Argyro had adhered like a limpet almost from the day of the funeral... No, it was before that. She had been there the first night, making coffee, washing up. Listening to Stamati's first rush of words, when he was angry that he had been left, abandoned by his wife and therefore by God. He had raged for those first few days and Argyro had not batted an eyelid. She had continued to come, to listen, to make food that was left uneaten, and pour coffee that went cold until the rage evaporated into silence and the coffee was drunk in spasmodic gulps and plain food was shovelled in with no pleasure. And there she had remained by his side, until the fog cleared enough for him to speak and she clung all the tighter.

'Being neighbourly,' Spiros had heard her tell enquirers.

'Go to hell!' he shouted across the water to her.

And there was something neither she nor his baba was saying, that had something to do with his grandfather. What in heaven's name did his grandfather have to do with Baba marrying Argyro and putting up with her unpleasant and bullying ways?

'Go to hell and back!' he shouted, even louder, but the wind whipped his words away. He sat for what seemed like hours, watching the lights on the island go out one by one until only the dotted street lights were left. He counted them – twelve – across the whole of the town. He counted them again, to pass more time because he had no idea what he was going to do.

When morning came, after a disturbed and uncomfortable night, his anger still raged but a solution was not forthcoming. But one thing he did know, he could not face going back. He would be like a dog with his tail between his legs and she would be stronger than ever. No, he was not going back. So he splashed his face with seawater and set off, with no clear aim or direction. At first he walked, one foot in front of the other along the cracked tarmac lane, noting the weeds that broke through at the edges, wiping his neck as the sun caused him to sweat. Soon the narrow lane joined a wider road, and a farmer stopped and offered a lift in his battered truck. Spiros hopped on board, indifferent to where they were going, but glad to have the speed of his travels change to break the monotony. There were more lifts – and more walking – but none of it mattered much. He slept by the roadside and ate what was offered by kind people he met. When the third evening came, he was in no better position than he had been the day he left – just further from the sea and more hungry. But he cared little about either.

That evening he found himself in a village made up of a tiny gathering of cottages. The nearness of so many people brought back memories of his friends on the island and he yearned for a little company. But, as twilight settled, the inhabitants shut their doors against him and all became silent, and he felt very alone. He slept under an olive tree, the twisted roots curled around him, the warm ground holding him. He slept deeply and dreamlessly, grateful to sink into oblivion.

He was woken in the morning by a dog licking his face.

'Go away.' He pushed at the dog, but the animal was insistent and so he scratched it behind its ears and it twisted and whined in ecstasy. Soon the dog ran off, and Spiros had a raging thirst. The village would have water, but he hesitated, recalling the closed shutters and doors from the night before. The place felt unfriendly, and the little pride he had left made him reluctant to return.

Up ahead, the dog yelped.

The way it was going, there was a definite track but it appeared to lead into the hills. Better to go back down to the road and move onward.

The dog yelped again and came hurrying back towards him, tail down, expressing a sense of urgency.

'Here, boy – here!' he called, but the dog ran off again, looking back and yelping. It was odd, not a natural way for a dog to behave, so he followed. The olive trees ended at a rocky outcrop and the dog dodged around behind the boulders. Spiros followed, and there, between two large rocks, a cottage nestled – whitewashed, with a burnt-orange tiled roof and bushes of flowers in pink, white and pale orange softening the edges. The dog stood at the door, whining.

'*Yeia sas*?' Spiros called. 'Anyone here?' and he moved closer to the doorway. The dog ran inside.

'Hello?' he repeated, and was answered by a weak moan, a sound of pain. He stepped into the cottage and was on his hands and knees within seconds to aid the white-haired lady sprawled on the floor.

'Who's that?' she said, through dried lips.

'Wait, I will get you water.' By the deep, stained and scratched marble sink was a pump, and with minimal movement he grabbed a glass and filled it, the dog nudging him to one side to drink the overspill.

'Here you are.' He put the glass to her lips and she sipped slowly. It brought back memories of nursing his mama in her last days and, although he would not have wished this old lady to suffer, he acknowledged to himself that it gave him comfort to care for her like this.

Time passed, but he had no idea how long he was there. An hour? Two? He sat as still as he could, giving the old lady sips of water. The cottage was small and dimly lit, but by now his eyes had become accustomed to the gloom. There was a giant wooden dresser, painted white, and now peeling, adorned with three brown bowls and a clock that had stopped. The old lady's upright chair by the open fire softened with a hand-crafted cushion that had faded and sagged with age. A narrow bed, in the corner of the room, was neatly made. Occasionally, dust fell from the ancient roof tiles that were exposed above the rough timbers. The quiet was punctuated at intervals with the sounds of small animals scratching.

After some time the woman felt revived enough to try sitting. She seemed more comfortable now, and she drank greedily. Spiros was relieved to see the colour returning to her cheeks.

71

'Who are you?' she finally asked, and although he had had no intention of telling her anything, somehow the whole story spluttered out. At the end she gave him a sympathetic look and said, 'I think I've twisted my ankle. Seeing as you have no place to go and nothing to do, you may stay here. The donkey has been gone for some years now so you can have his shed.'

Helping her to her chair, he asked if she needed a doctor.

'What, so he can take money I do not have?' she scoffed.

'Is there anyone in the village you would like to come?'

'The village? That bunch of inbred idiots! Why would I want any of them to come?' she had sneered, and so they continued to sit until the sun went down. Later, after they had shared some feta and a handful of figs, he helped her to bed and then went out to discover the barn, where a soft pile of straw awaited him.

Chapter 10

The following day he tapped at the cottage door and peeped around it, expecting the woman to still be sleeping, but she was up and using an upturned brush as a crutch.

'Morning,' she chuckled, 'did the mice bite your toes?

He looked down at his feet, at the holes in his socks, and laughed and nodded his head. 'I've not been out to collect the eggs so these are yesterday's,' she announced. Next to the sink under the only window in the room was a wooden table on which was perched a single-burner gas stove. A *briki* was boiling away fiercely, the eggs bouncing to the top and sinking again.

'Shall I do that?' he suggested. 'The less weight you put on your ankle, the quicker it will heal.'

'True, true,' she had said and she hobbled gratefully to the lone chair. 'There is yesterday's bread as well, in the *fanari*. I don't bake every day now, it's such a fuss getting the oven up to temperature.' She looked out of the window, and Spiros followed her gaze to the traditional domed bread oven outside, partly obscured by a mass of geraniums.

'You have everything you need, eh?' he said by way of conversation and took the bread out of the mesh cage hanging from the ceiling. The hopeful flies, unable to penetrate its fine gauze and disturbed by Spiros, buzzed round the room and out of the door, beckoned by the sun.

'There is a table round the side,' she said. In the light of day he could see the old woman had a kind face; her voice was gentle and there was something very motherly about her.

As she had suggested, the table was around the far side of the cottage, scrubbed and worn smooth with age, and alongside it was a second wooden chair, and he brought both indoors. The old woman had very little by way of crockery and cutlery, and what she had was in the sink. He cranked the pump, creating a spray, and the sun that streamed through the window above the sink caught the droplets in its light and created a rainbow. As he worked he played with the prism effect, taking his time over a simple job.

The old lady watched him, and when all was ready they sat together and ate. The eggs were so fresh it seemed there were hints of the herbs the chickens had been eating.

'I am Spiros, by the way,' he said through mouthfuls of crusty bread that had been dipped into his egg.

'And I am Leontia,'

He blinked; he had never heard of such a name.

'It is an old Byzantine name from Constantinople, and I am very pleased to meet you.' And she gave a little bow, bending from the waist. The words were ready at the front of his mouth to tell her that it had not been Constantinople since 1928, that it was Istanbul now, but then most people on the Island still called it Constantinople.

The day passed amicably. Spiros helped her outside, where she gently gave him orders on how to tend her vegetable plot and asked him if he wouldn't mind clearing an area of stony ground where she wanted to plant courgettes. In his tending of the plants he learned a lot. Accompanying each plant was a narration from Leontia about the amount of water it liked and when. She said that some plants preferred to be watered at night, others in the morning, that some needed shade in the long, hot days, and that others thrived in the heat of the sun. She told him of the changes to the forms and internal textures that had occurred through the months as each plant had grown, and how, from watching her crop so carefully, she knew the perfect time to harvest each one. As well as learning about the plants, Leontia reminded Spiros that there was a way you could ask someone to do what was needed without being aggressive and dismissive like Argyro. But, more than anything, Spiros worked up an appetite.

'Can I cook some food?' he asked.

'Well, we have what is all around us on the bushes and in the ground, although there is a little food storage cupboard inside under the sink.' She paused to pat the dog's head. 'The marble and the running water keep the temperature slightly lower there,' she added by way of explanation.

Spiros delighted in making for Leontia a simple dish of beans in a red sauce, the way his mama had taught him, and he swore to himself it was the most delicious food he had ever tasted.

Leontia declared it was alright, and after that she ate without comment for the next few days. During those days they set up a pleasant routine. She would sit in the house and give him instructions on what needed doing there, or she would sit outside and give instructions concerning the garden. He even repositioned some of the slipped tiles on the roof. Spiros found he enjoyed physical work and, although he went to bed aching in limb and muscle, he felt satisfied, and more importantly he felt needed.

At the end of three days, Leontia declared she would try her ankle a little.

'I'm not sure that's a good idea,' Spiros said.

'Nonsense. I have to try it some time. Come here and be my support.' And, between the two of them, they got her unsteadily onto her feet.

'I will walk to the bush with the pink flowers. Come, help me.' They walked together, side by side, with Spiros supporting her weight, and when she got to the flowers she picked one and put it in her fuzzy white hair. To Spiros it looked funny and charming at the same time, and caused him to look rather more closely. She had clearly once been a good-looking woman, and he wondered if she would tell him about herself if he asked. For instance, why did such a lovely person live alone and why did she want nothing to do with the villagers?

'Now, I have walked five steps so we must celebrate,' she announced, and he helped her back to the house. She went in alone and returned with a handful of drachmas.

'Here, go to the village. They have a market today,' and then she told him what to bring her. The spices she listed were unfamiliar to him.

When he returned he found she had been busy: she had lit a fire outside and spread the embers and had several pots bubbling.

'Welcome home.' She greeted him with a smile and, although her calling this place his home made him feel welcome and wanted, it also unsettled him. Was it his home now? When his mama was alive she had made their house his home; she hugged him like she needed him, like he was the air she breathed. He had always felt loved. He still felt loved by his baba but he did not feel needed. That was the difference. Here, with Leontia, he felt needed again.

Leontia took the various things he had bought, added pinches of this and that to her pots and replaced lids, and the smells became amazing, intoxicating, fascinating.

When he tried to lift the lids to better smell the aromas she tapped his hands away with her wooden spoon and her eyes glinted as if she was in the middle of mischief.

When served, the dishes were such as he had never tasted before, and with a proud look in her eye she declared that her grandmother had been French but, more importantly, her family came from Constantinople. 'Where they can really cook,' she added, with a dismissive glance in the direction of the village.

'What happened between you and the village?' Spiros asked, a forkful of asparagus in the lightest lemon sauce he had ever tasted poised before his lips.

'Arrogant, insular thugs,' she answered. 'And the *kafeneio* owner is a treacherous…' She finished her sentence with a word he had not often heard before and he looked at her wide-eyed and shocked.

'Ha!' she cried. 'You think the old cannot swear as well as the young! Serve me some more, would you.' And that was all that was said about why she lived on the fringe of the village.

When their stomachs were full and the dog was curled up with its tail over its nose they sat and watched the last of the daylight merge into the night.

'My mama cooked.' Up until then he had always thought hers was the best cooking in the world, but now, with his eyes opened a little, he realised that maybe she had been provincial, at least in culinary terms.

'Yes, you said,' Leontia replied.

'She was good, but that was better.' He felt like a traitor, but he could not deny the truth.

The jasmine beside the cottage was releasing its evening scent, and the last of the embers glowed in the fire.

'Will you teach me?' he asked.

'Most of my recipes have been passed down from mother to daughter. There are secrets in them we have not shared for generations,' Leontia said, and she settled back in her chair as if about to tell a story. Her fuzzy white halo of hair reflected the bright moonlight and, behind her, the lime-washed cottage glowed between the dark sentinels of rock. It was a beautiful sight, but the whole scene was a little odd, too – mysterious, somehow.

'I was married, you know,' Leontia said.

'No, you did not say.'

'Well, I was. To a man from that village. I did not meet him there, needless to say, I met him in Saros. My family ran the best taverna in town there. Do you know Saros town?' Spiros shook his head.

'Well, he courted me and we married and he brought me here. Well, not here to this cottage. He brought me to the village, to his house there, behind the *kafeneio*.'

The memories appeared to be distressing her.

'You don't have to tell me.'

'Ah, but I think I do. I think I need to tell someone. I think I need to hear it out loud. I have a feeling I've been a very silly and petty woman and it has cost me dearly.'

'Then tell me, Leontia.' Spiros was sitting on the floor and he shuffled a little nearer to her feet.

'Well, he got me back to this tiny little village and I found that everyone who lived here, who lives there, is a relation of his. Not distant cousins but first cousins, sisters, uncles, close relations, and they did very little to make me feel welcome. So Vasilis, my husband, on that very first day of our arrival, announced I could cook and that they would all be welcome to come for a meal that night and I found myself cooking for a hundred and fifty people I did not know – nor, judging by the way they greeted me, had any reason to like.'

Spiros watched the last of the embers glowing and dying as she spoke. The coals glowed bright orange as the breeze caught them and then black as it dropped.

'Well, they ate and they said it was heavenly. But they said it to Vasilis, not me, and they declared his troubles were over. He could open a taverna and people from the villages all around would come and he could buy their produce. He would also need waiters and people to wash up, maybe someone to prepare the food for the cook. It seemed as if they all thought their troubles would be over with the opening of a single taverna. But no one spoke to me. They toasted Vasilis and they toasted their future and I felt like an outsider so I went to bed.'

Spiros could all too well identify with her loneliness, that feeling of being pushed out.

'Go on,' he encouraged her.

'Well, of course, Vasilis came to bed very pleased with himself and quite drunk on *tsipouro*, so I pretended to be asleep. The man who had courted me seemed to have disappeared and I was left with this brash, overconfident villager. The next day he was in a very good mood and he told me the plan that his family had dreamt up. It was better to keep the *kafeneio*, as it made some money, so they would use his cousin Yorgo's house, which was the next most central one in the square. Yorgos could move in with us until a new house was built for him, and in his house we would open a taverna, and people would come from miles to eat. Do you know what he said then, straight to my face?'

'What?'

'He said that marrying me had been the smartest move of his life.' Spiros could hear the tension in her voice. 'And his words made me feel like a pawn in his game, and I looked back over his courtship, and all that I had seen as romantic and proof of his interest in me I then saw as hollow acts designed to bring him to that very moment, and my love turned, just like that.' She snapped her fingers, but they hardly made a noise. 'Into hate.'

'Didn't you want to run a taverna?' He was not sure what to say. The power of the emotion running through her made him feel a little afraid.

'I realised I was stuck with him. After all, we were married... And I actually had no problem running a taverna – why not, I thought? But, as far as he was concerned, he was the big Vasilis, *kafeneio* owner, and no wife of his was going to work. No! He said I was to teach his unmarried cousins and *they* would do the cooking and serving and we, or rather he, would just manage it all.'

Spiros frowned into the darkness. It did all seem a little presumptuous of Vasilis, but what was so bad about putting her feet up and letting others do the work?

'I mean, these were recipes my family had protected for generations, right back from when my ancestors had the best taverna in Constantinople, and we were famed for our cooking. And he wanted me to give up these recipes, to actually teach them to a bunch of young girls I had never met before, on his say-so, without a "do you mind?"or a "please". There was no respect, Spiro, none at all.'

Spiros bristled, a heavy breath accompanying a flex of his shoulders, as the weight of Argyro's dominance still lingered there. He made a noise between a hum and a grunt, a sound that told her that he not only understood but also sympathised.

'So what happened?' he asked.

'Well, to cut a long story short, I refused. As you can imagine, Vasilis was not at all pleased. His taverna idea was going to save his whole family from their dependence on the turn of the weather and their crops. The frosts are harsh this high up. He was the man of the village and his little wife was showing him up. At least, that is what he said.' She paused and sighed heavily.

'But it was the way he did it, do you see? Maybe if he had asked me kindly, or included me in the idea, asked me to be the cook, even, maybe it would all have been different. In fact, I know it would all have been different.'

Spiros looked around him and wondered how she ended up here.

'Did he die?' he asked, and then realised it was a tactless question and stumbled to soften it. 'I mean, is he...'

'Die! No. He is still there, running his *kafeneio*.'

'And you are here?' Spiros looked up at her profile.

'Well, he thought he could persuade me with the back of his hand, so I hit him with the end of the broom. The broom got snapped over his knee and he came at me with one end so I clonked him on the head with a pan.'

She chuckled, but it was not a happy sound, and Spiros did not join in.

'So, as he sprawled on the floor moaning and trying to get to his feet, I ran. I ran to the donkey barn, which is your room now. The house was full of straw back then. And I hid.'

'You must have been terrified. Why didn't you go back to – where was it, to Saros, to your family?'

'Oh, you just didn't in those days. Once you were married that was it. You told your mama your husband was beating you and she would look at you as if to say, "What can I do? Your place is with your husband." I have heard this said. I only hope things are different now.'

'But he must know you are here now.'

'Of course he knows I am here now. He sells my eggs to the villagers, in his *kafeneio*.'

'So everything is alright, then?'

'He asked me back. Years and years ago. He did ask. But I had been living here for

85

months by then, I had managed through a winter. I knew he knew I was here, because a friend of his came to the olive grove with his goats and he had seen me several times. But when Vasilis came I thought he had come to beat me again so I hid. He went away and next time he came with two chairs and a table and that little bed. I still hid, though. He is a big man. So he spoke out loud, to the trees, to the breeze, and asked me back.'

'You didn't want to go?'

'What kind of man leaves a woman on her own through a winter up here? This is not sea level. We are in the mountains, the winters are harsh, the frost bites. I was angry at him.' She paused. 'And now I am old enough to have mellowed, but also old enough not to want change. I am settled here and he is settled there. I have been too long alone. I could not live with someone now. It is all too late.' She spoke with energy and then her head dropped as if the fight had left her. 'And I look at what I have and what I have not got and I wonder if I have been a petty, stubborn woman.'

'You have everything here,' Spiros said.

'Do I?' she asked and her hand reached out and ruffled his hair as if he was just a boy, and he understood.

'But in all the years that have passed you must have spoken to him, talked about all that happened, found some common ground at some point?'

'You would think so, wouldn't you? But the funny thing is that every time we talked the emotions rose up and it was as if the argument was fresh all over again, even fifty years later. I think our memories forget so many things. Names, places, conversations, but we never seem to forget emotions. They come back fresh and new, time after time.'

Spiros was distressed, hearing her say she felt petty and stubborn. Had she not told him that her husband had been consistently rude and unkind to her and even threatened her with violence? It made him consider the way Argyro spoke to him. It was all about the way she said things. If she asked, like Leontia did, he would do all she wanted in a flash because he would want to – but the way Argyro spoke! He involuntarily shuddered. Yes, he could see how Leontia could end up here all her life. Ha! And he was no different. He had ended up here, too, for similar reasons.

'We are the same,' he said.

'I know,' she answered and she ruffled his hair again, and this time he did not mind.

Chapter 11

That night's conversation changed things between them. The next morning she darned his socks, and slowly they both allowed her to act more like a mama towards him and he grew ever fonder of her.

The next few months were a delight of eating and learning to cook and, on one occasion, whilst they cooked, she told him that he was her heir. But he had already realised that. After stating it out loud, she seemed desperate to pass on her knowledge, but as the days passed she became more relaxed and they laughed a lot. Her ankle got steadily better and their friendship grew stronger by the day. They worked side by side in the vegetable garden, and, under her direction, he carried out a great deal of maintenance work around the cottage, making sure it would no longer leak or let in the cold winds in the winter. Then they set about making it harder for the mice to find a way in. Spiros mixed buckets of mud to block up the holes in the walls, and had begun smearing it into the first crevice when the woman had thrown handfuls of crushed garlic into the mix.

'A guarantee.' She had chuckled. 'They may scratch through mud and gnaw through wood but they will never eat their way through garlic!' The house had smelt of garlic for days.

Together they bound the straw in the donkey shed and covered it with a sheet. She swept the floor and he fixed the door. They talked little, smiled a lot and cooked small exquisite dishes three times a day.

He was happy and, as with all happy situations, the time passed by very quickly. Summer turned to winter and they congratulated themselves on the absence of mice. As it got colder they dragged his straw mattress into the main cottage to put it before the fire.

As night rolled in they would wish each other good night.

'Good night, Spiro,' she would say.

'Sleep well, Leontia,' he would reply, and then they would listen to the night sounds and float off to sleep.

On one such night they had settled down as usual.

Good night, Spiro,' she called from her narrow bed. He was particularly tired that night and he replied, 'Sleep well, Mama' – and the night sounds were overlaid with a tension as they tried to fall asleep.

The following morning, Leontia said nothing and Spiros decided it was probably best to ignore his mistake, too. They worked hard through the morning and it was with relief that they sat down to a bite to eat in the afternoon. But no sooner were they sitting than Leontia's voice became low and serious.

'Spiro, I have made mistakes in my life and now it's too late to make them right. But it is not too late for you. I enjoy you being here, you know I do. I have grown to love you, and I have become lazy and now I even need you, but I will be no substitute.'

'Substitute?' He did not understand.

'You lost your mama and you gained a step-mama you do not get on with. You ran away' – he began to object but she put up a silencing hand – 'you ran away and found me here, and I am not the step-mama, but I have become a substitute for your real mama.'

'And what is wrong with that? She is dead.' Spiros did not like this conversation.

'Yes, she is dead, and I'm sorry for that. But your baba is not, and by making me into a substitute you are choosing between me and your baba, and I wonder how much by choosing me you are punishing him for his choice of new wife?' He began to object again, but again she silenced him, this time with a look that said she was not finished. 'I would like you to go home. Go home and sort your relationships out. Then, if you want to come back here you will be coming because you want to, and not because you are running away and hiding. Like I did.'

The idea came as a shock. Go back? Go and deal with Argyro. Make his peace? But as the idea percolated through his mind he began to miss his baba and to feel sad for the pain he was causing him. His baba had no idea if he was dead or alive, and that seemed a cruel punishment for taking a wife who could not hold her tongue. He didn't want it to be so but he knew Leontia was right. He might not make peace with Argyro but he should go back and make peace with his baba, or at least let him know he was alive and that he had a new life. So, with some reluctance, he agreed.

Deciding when he should return was the difficulty. There was one more dish she wanted to teach him, one more crop of vegetables he wanted to see ripen... Then the summer had passed and they were at the beginning of a second winter and she caught a cold. He could not leave then – she needed him.

The cold grew a little worse and because he did not know what to do Spiros begged her to let him get a doctor, someone to help from the village, but she laughed and coughed and told him to get out the box of pomegranates they were storing. From them she told him how to make a juice.

'It is full of goodness,' she said. 'It is full of antioxidants. Have you ever heard of them?' Spiros tutted his 'no' as he followed her instructions.

'More antioxidants in a pomegranate than any other fruit or vegetable we know. It won't get rid of my cold but it will speed my recovery,' she said as he offered her the pungent mix. She sipped it.

'Hmm, a little more orange juice next time,' she suggested, ever the cook.

'I will do it now.' He jumped up, intending to pick the juiciest orange he could find, straight off the tree.

'Please don't,' she begged. 'Just seeing your energy exhausts me.' He had never seen her so tired.

He continued to take care of her as they watched the spring arrive, bringing blossoms all around the cottage that promised the abundance of summer, and as the days grew longer Leontia grew in strength until she was her old self again.

One evening, when they could feel summer just around the corner, they sat down to an amazing dinner of roasted squash and potatoes in a fine light sauce that almost tingled on Spiro's tongue.

'You need to go home,' Leontia said quietly. 'I am well now.'

'But I am happy here.' His words were heartfelt and sincere and they came out fast.

'I am happier than I have ever been in many a year, but I am keeping you here. You are young, you have a life to lead. Maybe it is best if you go home, make your peace, and then you know that whatever you choose is actually a choice and not just a reaction to avoid what is unpleasant.'

The truth of what she said filled him with sadness. His baba still didn't know if he was alive or dead, and, if Spiros allowed himself to think of him, he missed him. He needed to return and make his peace with the whole situation.

'It is Friday, I believe,' she said. Spiros had lost track of the days of the week long ago. 'Monday is always a good day for a new beginning, so you will go on Monday.' He looked at her in disbelief, and opened his mouth to argue, but he could tell her mind was made up.

That evening, it had felt as if the parting was already happening. He hung on her every word and the next day he found reasons to work beside her.

'Do I really need to go?' he had asked.

'There is always a time to move on,' she said with a tiredness to her voice he had not heard before, and he wondered if he had outstayed his welcome.

On Saturday, they dragged his bed back to the donkey barn. She would not be able to do it after he had gone, she said; she no longer had the strength.

'Will you be happy when I decide to come back?' he asked.

'You may choose to stay,' she said, and her eyes moistened and she pulled him into a hug.

'I am so happy,' was all she said when they went to their beds that night.

The next day he was up with the cockerel as usual but Leontia, who was generally up before him, was not tending the vegetables, nor fixing the wall that they had started work on; nor was she up in the hills foraging for wild rocket and other foods. Maybe she had gone to the village. But that possibility was so unlikely he dismissed it. The dog was there, lying by her door, and as Spiros approached to pat its head it growled, something it had never done before. 'Quiet, dog,' he said, but a panic gripped his heart and he burst into the old lady's room.

She was there, on the bed, eyes closed, looking so peaceful, but no breath came or went and the dog crawled under the bed, whimpering. He looked at her face, her wrinkled skin all relaxed, and he could see the young woman she had once been. The smooth skin of her cheek, the curve of her jaw, the height of her brow were all still there, hinting at the days of energy and youth. He cried for her, he cried for her lost youth – the love she had never had, the fun she had never known, the children she had never borne – and for the reality that he would miss her, his friend. He also cried for his mama, for the times she would never know, the grandchildren she would so have like to have seen, and the abandonment he felt because she was not here to help him through this time, when her very presence would make Argyro disappear and make his baba content again, his old self. And he cried for himself, over the loss of his soft protector, his baba and his home and family, and over the long fingers of loneliness that stretched before him and clawed at his future.

Then he got up, went outside and, through blurred vision, tried to finish the wall they had begun as if this would fix the situation, as if this would heal his heart, bring life to the old lady's bones, return his mama to him and seal Argyro into the underworld. Soon he threw his tools to the floor and looked to the sky, taking a deep breath to calm his raising pulse. He picked some flowers and took them in to her, put them in her hand and kissed her cheek, which still held some warmth. His tears flowed anew and he let them. He let himself cry and moan and even howl like a dog for his loss. He told her how much he was going to miss her and he shouted at her for leaving him, but most of all he told her how much he loved her. When his emotions were temporarily spent, he brushed her hair across the pillow, said goodbye and firmly closed the door behind him.

The dog came when it was called and the two of them walked down to the village and up to the *kafeneio*. The dog sat waiting patiently outside whilst all eyes watched Spiros. He walked past the man who had given him a lift into the village the year before and straight up to the *kafeneio* owner, who was a wizened old man with a turned-down mouth and crooked hands. With a few simple words he explained to Vasilis that Leontia was gone and he watched as tears gathered in the old man's eyes. The old man made eye contact, briefly, and then his head dropped and his hands twisted on themselves. He turned without a word and disappeared through a back door.

As Spiros left the *kafeneio* and stepped back into the sunshine, he told the dog to stay, and it sat on the steps watching him go.

Only one man got up and stood by the door to watch him walk out of the village. It was the man who had given him the lift. When Spiros turned for a last look at the place he knew he would never visit again, the man on the steps waved, briefly, with hesitation, and then his hand dropped to rest on the dog's head.

Chapter 12

Vasso did her best to hide her tears and to sniff quietly. Her cheeks and her chin were wet and her hand was on his arm, the end of her fingers stroking and comforting. His hand was laid on hers and their fingers became interlocked.

'So then you came back,' she whispered.

'Then I intended to come back.' He released her hand and went into the taverna, coming out with a handful of paper napkins that he dabbed ineffectually at her cheeks and her eyes.

'But, as I wandered towards home' – he sat back down and looked away as she blew her nose – 'at the next village I was offered a job as a cook in a taverna and one thing led to another. I worked in six tavernas in different villages and towns as I headed back here. That took another year, but it was a good year and I learnt much about cooking for customers – timing the food, that sort of thing.' His voice trailed off.

'And still Argyro does not let you cook?'

'I came back expecting to turn the taverna around, but she won't even let me try. She said I had made my decision when I left and if I wanted a job I could have one as a waiter, at the usual waiter's pay.'

'Why is she so angry?' Vasso looked around for somewhere to put the used tissues but then scrunched them into a ball in her hand. 'So what will happen if she finds out about your lunchtime service?'

'I have no idea. I think it's unrealistic to hope she won't find out. I didn't really intend it. The first time I only cooked for Dimitri, who had turned up with a couple of fish. Then he told his friends but the quality of the food Argyro had in the fridge was so bad I told them I wouldn't cook. The next day they turned up with Ilias and his morning catch and a group of friends. That was only last week – and now see, all the island is here.' He sighed, but he was smiling. 'So you're right, she's bound to find out.' He sighed again but this time the smile had gone. 'I guess I will try to talk to her. If she listens and lets me cook then all my takings will go to the taverna. But if she doesn't listen then whatever I have made so far I will use to open my own taverna.'

'What? Here on the island? You want to open one here?'

'Yes, why not?'

'Yes, why not. Although... I don't know how these things are, but wouldn't that be a little bit like declaring war on Argyro? I mean, how would your baba feel?'

'To hell with him!' Spiro's chair toppled over backward as he stood and his voice was loud. Vasso put her hand to her mouth, wishing she hadn't spoken.

'Sorry, Vasso, I didn't mean to scare you.' He turned to her and bent his knees so his face was level with hers. One hand was on hers, and the other smoothed a wisp of hair from her brow.

'Did I tell you how beautiful you are?'

'Are you teasing me now?'

'No, I'm not teasing you.'

'I know I am plain.'

'It's true you don't curl your hair or cover yourself in make-up, but that is part of why you are beautiful. You're real. There's nothing fake or dishonest in your looks. You are natural and, although we are young, you remind me, in your nature, of the old woman.'

His face moved closer to hers and she was overcome with an urge to kiss him. His chin

100

extended forward and she knew she should draw away but she could not. The softness of the touch, the gentle brush of his lower lip on hers sent thrills like ice water down her spine and she involuntarily shivered, which made him stop, which left her both thankful and horrified.

'Are you alright?' His voice was a whisper, his face so close he was almost out of focus. Her throat closed and her stomach knotted. There was no way any words could be spoken but she managed the slightest nod of her head. He looked at her mouth and moved in again and this time they locked together, his hands in her hair, hers around his shoulders. Colours swam in her head, thrills chased each other through her body, her outer layer melted and she could have sworn that his did, too, and that they became one. Then from some dark, primal place deep inside her came urges that she had been warned all about, not only by her mama but by the priest, and she pulled away, her heart racing, eyes wide.

She must control herself. She must stop. But would he? If the tales told by the old women who gossiped in the village, or her friends at school, had any validity, he would, at best, persuade her to follow these urges now. At worst, he would force himself on her.

He smiled. He said nothing. He did nothing. He just smiled and looked in her eyes

101

and all her fears melted. But he did not try to kiss her again. Instead he stroked her hair.

'I'll go now,' he said. 'I'll lock the taverna doors but the side gate in the courtyard is open so you are not a prisoner.' He chuckled at his words.

Part of her wanted to pull him back, continue the adventure they were having. How could something that felt so perfect, so true, be considered wrong?

She lay a long time on her new bed, staring at the ceiling, playing the conversation and the events over in her mind. She stayed awake so long that by morning she was as tired as if she had not slept at all and Argyro had to come in and shake her by the toe.

'I hope you're not one of these people who can't get up in the morning?' she said, and bustled back to the taverna, stopping by the little table under the lemon tree and staring pointedly at the two glasses, before gathering them up with sharp movements, making the glasses ring so hard together that Vasso feared they would break.

Vasso hurriedly washed and dressed, but today she did not braid her hair tightly. She took a lock from either side of her face and twisted these behind her head so most of her hair fell free.

Stamatis gave her a warm smile as she came through the back door. She was glad it was dark inside as she felt the events of the night before must show on her face.

'You look happy,' he said, and offered her a coffee. Argyro was at the table by the counter, reading a magazine, drinking a coffee and smoking a cigarette; if Vasso accepted a coffee, would she have to sit at the table too?

'Morning!' Spiros bounced in full of energy and grinned widely at Vasso. Stamatis looked from him to Vasso and back and then a twinkle came to his eye.

'Two coffees here, son. Take them outside with you.' Stamatis controlled his smiles and offered the cups to Spiros, who took them, nodding his head towards the door where the sun beamed in, beckoning to Vasso to join him. Argyro did not look up.

Orino Island was already bustling. The cargo ship had its tailgate lowered onto the harbour side, and each swell of the calm sea raised the boat and lowered it, grinding the paint off the tailgate, tattooing the flagged stone quayside. Men with their shirts unbuttoned unloaded pallets of water bottles, boxes of flour and rice and pasta. A washing machine was hauled off, along with dozens of shoeboxes bound to each other with tape. On the quayside, surrounding the end of the boat, men with handcarts had gathered in a semicircle, yokes of rope attached to the handles over their shoulders to assist them with the heavier loads, and teams of donkeys, eyes closed, ears flicking at the early morning flies, waiting to be burdened. The man she had seen yesterday, with the sand-coloured hair and the fuzz of growth on his top lip, was amongst them. He was feeding his lead donkey an apple. The apple disappeared in a succession of quick bites and he leaned towards the beast and seemed to whisper something in its ear. The donkey raised and lowered its head, shaking at the halter. The man patted its neck.

'So, how are you this morning?' Spiros asked, and his hands crept across the table to take hers. She automatically drew them back and looked towards the taverna, but no one stood there watching them, and she let her hands return; he found them, his fingers exploring hers, her nails, her knuckles, the creases between her fingers, the mound of her thumb.

'I'm well. And you?' she managed.

Chuckling, he rolled his eyes. 'Very formal. Vasso, you *are* allowed to be excited. I assume you feel the same way as I do? Tell me I'm not mistaking the signals? Is it not that we have found each other? If you feel the same way, it is a miracle, we can celebrate!'

She expected to feel the usual heat in her cheeks at his words, but it did not come. Instead, she shuffled in her seat and her spine grew straight, her chin lifted, her neck elongated and she laughed with confidence.

'Vasso!' The sharp shriek could be no one else's and Vasso jumped from her chair to do Argyro's bidding. But no sooner was she inside than Argyro was outside and standing very close to Spiros. She seemed to be trying to speak quietly, but her words carried and Vasso looked away.

'Spiro, I do not pay either you or her' – she stabbed a nicotine-stained finger towards Vasso inside – 'to conduct a love affair in public. Besides, she is a nobody and it does not look well that you are amusing yourself with her.'

At this, Vasso took hold of the sink's edge to steady her swaying and sucked in air, trying not to faint. Was Argyro right? Was he toying with her?

'What are you saying, Argyro? She is a distant cousin, a relative of mine and Baba's. If you call her a nothing, you are calling your husband a nothing!'

'And I have told you, you call him Stamatis in public. Let us at least try to look professional.'

105

'Professional!' Spiro's voice began to rise.

'Don't you dare raise your voice to me!' Argyro hissed, and Vasso was afraid just witnessing the exchange.

'Argyro, my love...' Stamatis was outside on nimble feet, his arm around her shoulder but his eyes on Spiros, and Vasso could not tell whether, with that look, he was taking sides. His free hand reached out to touch Spiro's arm, and Vasso wondered if the fear in his eyes arose from the possibility that his son might leave again.

Just this touch seemed to infuriate Argyro.

'You always take his side,' she spat. 'You dote on him on purpose to remind me again and again of...' But she did not finish her sentence.

'No, no, no, no, Argyro!' Stamatis dropped his hand from Spiros and put both on her shoulders. She had all his attention now.

Out of the corner of her eye, Vasso noticed an old man tentatively take a seat just outside the door of the taverna. His attention was caught by the commotion and his jaw dropped open at the scene.

'And, when goading me with that does not work, then one of you' – she glared at Spiros – 'always manages to mention our grandfathers.'

106

'No one had mentioned–' Stamatis began.

'That's because this time I mentioned it first to take away your spiteful power.' Argyro pulled away from them both and stomped towards the taverna door. Vasso decided this was a good moment to use the bathroom.

'And where are you going?'

Vasso froze in her tracks and turned around to find with relief that it was not her that Argyro was addressing.

The old man who had only just sat down was making an attempt to leave but Argyro fixed her stare on him.

'Stamatis, we have a customer here. Get him a coffee.'

'Actually, I have just remembered an appointment,' mumbled the old man. He did not make eye contact.

'Then it is best you fortify yourself with coffee before you go. Stamatis, is the *briki* boiling?'

Vasso willed the old man to stick to his guns and leave, and she felt such a sinking in her stomach as he sat down again, muttering, 'Just for five minutes, then.'

Chapter 13

For the rest of the morning Vasso felt as if she were walking on glass. There were very few customers and consequently not much to do. Stamatis cast her a few sympathetic glances – when Argyro was not looking – and Spiros just smiled broadly but there seemed to be a sadness behind his grin.

She spent most of her time watching the cargo ship unload. Then the one-day-cruise ship arrived and there was a flood of Asian people-perhaps Japanese-in pristine clothes and wide hats, with flashing cameras. Unlike the European tourists, they wore long sleeves and long trousers despite the heat, apparently to protect themselves from the sun's rays, with little regard for comfort in the heat. A few sat for a drink, taking photographs of each other and anything around them. Very few ventured away from the port and none of them stayed to eat. They seemed amused by the cats that wound their way around the legs of the tables, begging for nonexistent scraps. After two hours, a low bass horn sounded from the bowels of the ship and the tourists gathered like chicks following a hen to head back to the gangplank. The vessel pulled away and Orino fell back into its usual calm. A donkey on the corner heaved its lonely cry, a bellow that faded into a wheezing whimper.

At last, Argyro and Stamatis wished them a good afternoon, and her round figure swayed after his thin stooping frame as he tiptoed to the turning, where they disappeared from sight.

'Right, I'm just off to the butchers,' said Spiros, watching them leave.

Vasso watched him go too. He neither tiptoed, nor swayed. He strode with authority and energy, purposeful.

From nowhere, a voice hissed in her ear, 'Where's Spiros going?' It was Argyro. Vasso jumped and put her hand to her heart.

'Oh, you made me jump,' was all she could think to say.

'Well, where is he going with such purpose?'

'Er, he didn't say. But he did mention he thought his hair was getting too long. So maybe…'

'Whatever. Where are my cigarettes?' Argyro headed inside.

'I'll get them.' Vasso trotted to the table inside and hurried back. The less time Argyro was there, the less chance there was of her seeing anything amiss.

'Here you are.'

'Hmm. Do you smoke?'

'No,'

'Hmm, I thought this was a full pack.'

'No, I don't smoke.' How dare Argyro accuse her? She would never take even a cigarette without asking.

'Oh, don't get all offended. I can't stand people who get offended.' And with these words she trundled off after Stamatis, who was waiting on the corner. Vasso waited anxiously, willing her to hurry. Spiros would be back in a moment and people were beginning to gather in groups of twos and threes on the walkway, glancing towards Argyro. As soon as she turned the corner these people descended on the tables and chairs, filling those nearest to the taverna door first.

Seconds later, in strode Spiros. There was no mistaking where he had been, the heavy plastic bags in his hand emblazoned with a motif of a bull and a sheep.

'She came back,' Vasso whispered as they went inside together.

110

'Who – Argyro? What for?'

'Her cigarettes.' Vasso's heart was still pounding but Spiros just shrugged and put the bags on the counter, and began to arrange his kitchen.

Dimitri came in rubbing his hands.

'Hello, my friends,' he called.

'*Yeia sou*, Dimitri,' Spiros returned. He was alive again, his eyes bright and his energy pouring into his work.

The lunch went well. Spiros grilled lamb, first flavouring the meat with lemons, garlic and oregano. The oregano was fresh from a bush in a corner of the courtyard, and he ground it in a marble mortar with a blunt, heavy pestle. The lemons, of course, came straight off the tree in the courtyard, and Vasso was tasked with skinning the garlic. Spiros showed her how to shake a whole garlic head between two metal bowls to skin all the cloves within seconds. He added one more element to this mix of flavours, teasing Vasso, saying it was a 'secret ingredient', and then rubbed the concoction onto the lamb before cooking it. The main dish was served with a salad of tomatoes, cucumber and coarsely chopped onion, topped with thick slices of feta and plenty of olive oil. The plates came back empty, wiped clean with hunks of bread.

111

Tired but happy, Spiros had a brief nap, and encouraged her to do the same when he got up, but she could not sleep for the excitement of it all, so she swilled her face with cool water instead. As she headed back to the taverna Spiros met her in the courtyard. His hand slipped around her waist and he pulled her in for a kiss that she could not resist.

'You are the girl for me,' he whispered. As quickly as it happened they parted and he was back outside, chatting to potential customers, drumming up trade.

Presently Argyro returned, and as soon as she put down her bag and lit up a cigarette she called them.

'Spiro, come in. Vasso, you too.' Her face was grim.

'I saw Kyria Papadopoulos on the way here,' she began, her voice turning sharp. 'She congratulated me on the trade we are doing.' Vasso felt her forehead turn cold. 'She seemed to think we were doing very well indeed, especially at lunchtime.'

She looked from Vasso to Spiros and back.

'Why would she say that?' Spiros asked.

'Yes, that is what I wondered. Why would she say such a thing? Is it, perhaps, that we have one or two customers you do not tell me about? Eh? Keep the money to yourself, perhaps?'

Vasso wanted to spit 'How dare you!' at her, but the woman's size alone scared her.

'Ah, but Kyria Papadopoulos does not know how organised you are.' Spiros seemed calm in his reply. 'You would know if I had served even one meal by what was missing from the fridges. Come, let us look.' And he made as if to head for the fridges.

'I do not need you to patronise me, Spiro.' Argyro tried to sound calm but there was now an inflection of uncertainty in her voice, and her neck took on a reddish tinge. 'I cannot believe that she would say such a thing without good reason.'

'I agree, it does sound strange,' Spiros replied and the two walked away from each other, leaving Vasso standing alone, a cold sweat on her brow. Argyro clearly believed something was going on, and she did not seem the sort to be satisfied before she had dug out the whole truth.

Later, when Argyro and Stamatis left for the night, Vasso was no less agitated. The calm everyone was displaying felt false, like the silence in the playground at school a second or two before the boys broke into a fight. The fear of what seemed inevitable kept adrenaline coursing through her all day and, by the time she and Spiros were alone, she felt exhausted, even though nothing more had happened.

'She might come back tomorrow, to try and catch you,' she ventured, hoping Spiros would say something to reassure her.

'Yes, I know,' he said, downing his first ouzo. Neither his words nor his drinking made her feel any less tense.

'Why don't you just cook her something, show her how good you are?'

'Because her mind is already made up.'

They were sitting under the lemon tree. Spiros tipped his head back. Vasso could not understand how he could be so calm.

'Look at the stars, Vasso,' he encouraged her, and she leaned back to look up at the sky. Immediately his hand came to her throat and trailed a line down to her collarbone. His lips descended on her so slowly she almost grabbed the back of his head and pulled him down to end the exquisite pain of the anticipation. But she controlled herself and waited, and the waiting made her yearn, yearn to be his everything. It seemed only a matter of time before she would lose herself to him, and somehow the right and the wrong of it all no longer seemed important.

Chapter 14

'I can't believe you're doing this, after yesterday!' Vasso exclaimed the next afternoon.

'Where do you want these?' Dimitri asked, holding up two carrier bags. They looked heavy. Argyro and Stamatis had only been gone five minutes and since then Spiros had been in the kitchen area, clearing and organising.

'Spiro?' Vasso leaned over the counter. 'Argyro suspects. I feel sure she'll come back. Why are you risking this?'

'Because I don't have enough money for a down payment for the rent of my own taverna yet.' He took a knife and began to sharpen it, the steel and the knife flashing back and forth, the sunlight through the doorway bouncing off the blade.

'But if she catches you, you still won't have enough money but nor will you have a job. Then where will we be?'

'We?' He stopped sharpening and grinned at her.

'Spiro, why aren't you taking this seriously?' Vasso implored.

His grin faded.

'I'm taking it very seriously. If she suspects, then she suspects. She may come back today, or maybe she will wait until tomorrow, or next week. Am I supposed to stop and lose all those days?'

'But to keep going as if nothing has happened the day after she mentioned it! Surely the biggest chance is that she will come today?'

'Or maybe she will be sneaky, think that we will expect her today and so come tomorrow. That is what I would do.'

'Spiro, I'm scared.' Vasso held in her breath, forced back the wave of emotions, denying the tears. At this, Spiros dropped both knife and sharpening steel to come out from behind the counter and put his arms around her shoulders.

'Ah, it was only a matter of time.' Dimitri came out of the bathroom, wiping his hands on his shorts. 'But maybe save that for later. Look, the tables are filling up.'

'Argyro knows.' Vasso unburied herself from Spiro's embrace, from his rich, musky scent.

'She knows!' All merriment was gone from Dimitri.

'She suspects,' Spiros clarified.

'You think she will come?'

Spiros shrugged.

'So, I can wait on the corner and give an alarm,' Dimitri suggested.

'And then?' Vasso asked. 'We are meant to hide everyone, wave a magic wand so everything is cleared away?'

'It was just a thought.'

Spiros had broken away and was back behind the counter, chopping and cooking.

'Ah, Vasso.' Dimitri folded his arms. 'The man cannot help himself.' They both watched Spiros.

By the time the first plates of food were ready, Vasso was still hovering nervously by the doorway, watching for Argyro.

At one point, a young boy who had been hanging a piece of string into the harbour's water, his spine visible through his dark brown thin skin, straightened up from his play, hitched up his oversized shorts and wandered over and asked her, in an disinterested way, what she was doing.

'I'm just watching out for someone,' Vasso replied.

'Who for?' the boy asked, but she did not answer, and he began to guess, naming people she had never heard of. But when he guessed 'Kyria Argyro' the truth must have shown on her face.

'She's scary,' the boy agreed, and made a grab for a kitten, ever hopeful of crumbs, winding its way between the tables.

Soon the food was ready, and Vasso took out plate after plate until everyone was served. She began to relax, and wondered if her fears were unfounded. Some of the customers had left and she had started clearing up when the boy who had chased the kitten came running up to her.

'She's coming,' he puffed. 'She's on the steps around the corner.' Vasso could practically feel the blood drain from her face at these words.

Running inside, she hissed at Spiros, 'She's coming, she's round the corner, on the steps.' How near or far this was she didn't know.

'*Gamoto!*' he swore. 'So the game is up!' And he threw the tea towel he was holding down onto the counter.

'Great food.' A man came in from outside. 'Bit short of cash today, I haven't been to the bank. Well, see you tomorrow.'

Dimitri put down his fork and sighed. 'Bad luck, Spiro,' he said. But Vasso was not sure she wanted to give up so easily.

'Clean up, I'll distract her,' she told them and ran from the taverna. The smooth flags were slippery and she could not run as fast as she would like. She rounded the corner and saw that, up ahead, the narrow path divided between the shops. To the left, the path continued level but, to the right, steps curled up and round the corner. She took these two at a time and at the top nearly collided with Argyro and Stamatis.

'Did you see him?' Vasso breathed heavily, panting for air. She exaggerated, wheezing, buying every second she could.

'See who?' Argyro asked, stopping in her tracks.

'He definitely came this way. I can't believe he isn't just here. He wasn't walking fast.' Vasso gasped between words, taking her time to speak.

'Who? Spiros?' Stamatis asked.

'No, not Spiros. A man who left without paying.'

'Someone left without paying?' Argyro's reaction was immediate and her face went red.

'Yes.' Vasso reached for the wall, making a barricade so they could not pass. 'But he wasn't moving fast so I think we could catch him.'

Behind Argyro the path divided again.

'Which way did you come? He must have gone the other way.' Vasso took a step towards them, not letting go of the wall, herding them back.

'The other way is a dead end,' Stamatis said.

'Then he is cornered. Come on.' And at Vasso's insistence they turned around and the three of them started back up the steps.

Vasso managed to keep up the search for some time, but her story sounded thin to her ears, and eventually they had exhausted all routes.

'Was he Greek or a tourist?' Argyro asked when they stopped.

'Dark-haired, maybe Greek, might have had an accent. I didn't really give him much notice.'

'Well, you should have. That's your job, to give customers attention. In my position what would you do? Would you pay for the mistake of the member of staff or suggest it should come out of the wages of the person who was responsible?' Argyro asked.

'I'm not sure that is fair, my love,' Stamatis interrupted. But at a glance from Argyro he fell silent.

'How much did he owe?'

'Oh, it was only a coffee,' Vasso said.

'What?' Argyro screeched. Stamatis winced at the sound. 'You mean we've been running all over town in this heat for a few drachmas!'

'It's the principle,' Vasso ventured.

'In this heat there are no principles,' the woman grumbled, calming down a little.

'But if one person does it then others may think they can try…'

But Argyro had finished talking and, with a heavy tread, she headed down towards the port. Vasso tried to estimate how long she had been able to delay them. If Dimitri and Spiros were quick, if people had not lingered over their meal, they could have done it. As they turned the corner into the port Vasso was ready for the taverna still to be a bustling hub of activity. But, with relief, she found everything calm. Dimitri was nowhere to be seen and inside all was cleared and Spiros was sitting at the table, his arms folded on its top, his head on his arms and his gentle breathing suggesting he was asleep.

'Well!' Argyro exclaimed. 'He does not seem too bothered about this person who could not pay,' she said.

'Well, no, he was asleep. He will know nothing about it,' Vasso said.

Argyro looked from Spiros to Vasso and back, as if deciding what to do. 'I wonder,' she said, 'if there was another reason you took me on that merry dance, and there was no old man who left without paying...' Vasso's face coloured at this, and Argyro nodded slowly. 'I've got your little game,' she continued. 'Your boyfriend here is asleep on the job again, and you didn't want me to see. Well, it will take more to fool me!'

Chapter 15

The stars above the lemon tree seemed even brighter that night.

Spiros mixed a little ouzo into a glass of water – 'just to give it flavour' – and offered it to Vasso.

'You took a really big risk today.' She sipped and licked her lips before drinking again. The taste was not unpleasant. Spiro's ouzo was neat, clear and clinging to the glass.

'Yes, probably – but you know, what's the worst that could happen?' He checked his breast pocket, where the wad of drachmas was safely folded away.

'She could sack you! Which would not only leave you without an income, but it would break your baba's heart.' Vasso took another sip. She could see why Spiros liked ouzo. Ice would make it even better.

'Where are you going?' Spiros asked.

'To get some ice.'

'I'll go.' He jumped up and was back within seconds.

'He is really torn, isn't he, your baba? I can see it on his face. He wants to take your side but it's like he owes Argyro, or he pities her, or something. That, and – if you don't mind me saying, and I completely understand – he is afraid of her.'

'There is something,' Spiros agreed. 'I've tried to talk to him about it but he just closes up. He's not one to discuss something he thinks he can do nothing about. That's why he never talks about politics or religion or anything like that. He doubts his ability to speak clearly and he believes whatever he says will make no difference anyway.'

They sat side by side looking up at the stars. The slight evening breeze ruffled the leaves of the lemon tree, which rubbed one against another as if they were passing on secrets.

'At one time, when I was cross, I accused him of marrying her for her dowry. I wasn't serious, but I said her dowry must have been very significant to make it worthwhile. He just told me it was none of my business. But some time later he said she had no dowry. He said she had nothing, and he said it like it was his fault.'

His hand crossed the small gap between them, searching for hers, and her breath came in rapid gulps.

'Ah!' she exclaimed. 'I've got it!'

'What?' Spiros turned from stargazing to look into her eyes, delighting in her sudden animation.

'That's it. I have the solution. You could have the down payment and the rent for a taverna of your own if you use my dowry.' She stared at him, and his eyes were all liquid in the half-light. She would have loved to have fallen in, like swimming in chocolate in the moonlight, warm and silky.

'Er, what are you saying!' Spiros smiled but he also frowned. 'Are you suggesting that we…?'

Vasso realised what she had just said and her hands darted to her face to cover her burning cheeks. Dropping her head, she could not meet his eye. What was she thinking, to say such a thing?

'Hey, don't be embarrassed. You just beat me to it.' He was laughing now, but the frown was still there.

'Sorry – it just popped out as the only solution I could think of.'

'And it's the perfect solution.' His arms were around her neck, his mouth so close. He looked into her eyes as if he could see the bottom of her soul. In turn, she could not control her response, her spine twisting, her whole body wriggling. He leaned towards her, so close, but there was no kiss.

'Shall we seal the deal?' he whispered, and every nerve in Vasso's body thrilled with the knowledge that they must be engaged now. She did not answer him, but his mouth met hers and she was lost.

In the small hours of the morning he woke her.

'Vasso, my baby, I must go.'

She reached for him, to draw him near again.

'Why must you go?' she murmured.

'Because it's not official yet. We must consider how it is seen. Tomorrow we will buy a ring, then the tongues will not wag.'

She was awake now, longing for him to stay.

'Besides, this is a delicious time, we must not rush it.' He kissed her and he still tasted of ouzo. It was indeed a most delicious time. One more kiss and he was gone, out of the side gate and into the night, leaving her running her hands over her body, remembering all the sensations he had created in her. She fell asleep smiling.

The next day he was in early. Argyro came in after him and, once she arrived, he said that he had something to do and that, seeing as he had been in early, he would take five minute's leave. She hardly looked up from her magazine.

He was longer than five minutes but when he returned he sidled up to Vasso, took hold of her left hand and slid on a ring that glinted in the sun.

'Do you like it?' he whispered.

'I love it,' she whispered back. It was very small but to Vasso it was perfect.

'Vasso! Spiro! I think I have mentioned that it does not look right, you two behaving in that way in such a public display.' Argyro's voice boomed out loud and strong.

'Ah, leave them, Argyro – they are young,' Stamatis said quietly.

'What are you saying, Stamatis? That it is alright for someone in this business to show the public that he can behave as he likes with a hired waitress? How does that look for our taverna?'

'I'm not so sure it matters like it once did,' Stamatis said, but there was little power in his voice.

'Well, I will not put up with it! It's shameful,' she snapped. 'Have you no shame, Spiro?'

'And why should I be ashamed?' Spiro's tone was light, goading.

'It's just not done, unmarried couples behaving in public in such a way!' Argyro's voice was growing steadily louder, but Spiros was calm, almost as if he was enjoying himself.

'Ah, well, there is the thing.' Spiros smiled.

'Thing? What thing?' She had discarded her cigarette and was standing legs apart, hands on hips, as if ready for a fight.

'The thing is, we are engaged.'

The silence that followed was intense.

Stamatis was the first to speak. 'Ah, my boy, congratulations.' He stumbled from behind the counter in his haste, and shook Spiro's hand enthusiastically then pulled him into a bear hug. Soon he released him, only to hug Vasso. 'My son has good taste,' he said, just loudly enough for her alone to hear.

'Engaged! You have known her a day!'

'Two,' Spiros taunted. 'But some things in life you just know.'

'Ridiculous,' his stepmother sneered. 'I will not put up with this.'

'There is nothing you can do about it! Oh, a customer, excuse me.' And he went outside, leaving Argyro sneering into Vasso's face.

'What kind of girl would get engaged after two days?' The corners of her mouth curled down and her upper lips wrinkled into her nose. Vasso struggled to see what kindly old Stamatis could ever have seen in her.

'I won't have it!' she snorted.

Vasso wanted to say that there was little that she could do about it, but she didn't. She held her tongue. Besides, her throat felt so tight she doubted she could utter a word.

'Stamatis, are you going to allow this?'

'Well, I don't really see that it is any of our business, Argyro my love. And Vasso here seems like a very nice girl to me. Her mama, I know, is a very good woman.'

'You have done enough for that woman already,' Argyro hissed.

Vasso, who had been looking at Stamatis, quickly turned to Argyro.

'What do you mean?' She could not be sure if she said these words or just thought them. The rushing of blood to her head made her ears sing; the floor moved slightly, undulated like the sea, and it occurred to her that she might faint, so she put her hand out to hold on to the counter's edge. She did not find the painted wood. Instead her hand was in Stamati's. He held her steady.

'She means nothing, Vasso. She is talking from anger.'

'I am not! How do you think your mama got by after your baba drank himself to death?' Argyro's face was contorted in her rage and her eyes were wide, red veins visible in the whites.

Vasso lost focus and the room span. She was going to fall but someone had hold of her. A hand encircled her waist, keeping her upright.

'This kind-hearted old fool, that's how!' Argyro spat. 'Why do you think you are here, eh? You don't think there aren't a dozen girls who would welcome working for us here on Orino Island? Of course there are. It's only because your mama owes us, that's why. And do you know what price we negotiated with your mama for your services this summer? Zero. Did you hear that? Zero, that's what you are worth.'

'No – Argyro you have gone too far...' Stamatis voice drifted.

Then the world really did start to spin and the edges went black and then red and then something hit her hip – or her legs gave way and she hit the floor. Either way she did not care. Instead, she willed the darkness to blot out everything as she let go.

Chapter 16

The world was underwater again. The sounds distorted, her vision blurred and she recognised that she had fainted – again. For a moment she remained still, trying to remember what had caused this second embarrassment, and with a rush the situation returned to her and she willed the blackness to come over her again. She wanted to be at home, to hear her mama deny that she had given her services for free to pay back an old debt to this horrible woman.

'Vasso, hey Vasso?' It was Spiro's voice. Or was it Stamati's?

'Take a sip.'

A glass was at her lips and she recognised the smell of ouzo. The smallest nip brought reality flooding back and her instinct was to run, to get away. Her legs scrambled backward, her feet slipping on the floor. Arms locked around her.

'It's ok. Shhh, Vasso my sweet.'

The arms remained and someone else took one of her hands, stroking across her knuckles: a tender, loving gesture. The mist across her eyes cleared and she found those tender touches were Stamati's and the arms around her Spiro's. There was no sign of Argyro. Looking into Stamati's kind face, she could believe that he would have helped her mama out. If he had, she would be more than pleased to return the favour – but to be spoken to like Argyro had spoken to her!

'Vasso, are you hearing me clearly? Argyro was wrong. I have agreed a wage with your mama for you to help out here. Only I thought it best not to tell her, because, well…'

There was no need for Stamatis to say any more. She understood.

'She was also wrong to speak to you like that.' His touch on her hand was so gentle. Spiros was kissing her hair, holding her close.

'Where is she?' Vasso asked, her voice betraying the tremble she felt inside.

'She's gone to buy her magazine,' Spiros said.

'Vasso, I would not be surprised if you wanted to go home now, after this,' Stamatis said, and Spiro's arms around her became tense,

133

more protective. 'But I will talk to her. So, for the sake of my son, if you can, please stay.'

'If Vasso goes, I go.' Spiros informed him.

'Yes, I know, I realised that. Let me talk to her.' Spiros patted Vasso's hand and stood, looked down on them both for a moment, and then walked out of the taverna in the direction of the magazine shop.

'Are you alright?' Spiros asked.

'I've never come across such a woman. She is so cold, so hard, so cruel.' Vasso would have liked to go home, back to the village, to be with her mama. But if she went, what would happen to her and Spiros? He said he would follow her, but to take him away from Stamatis? Also, there were no jobs in her village – maybe he could find a job nearby, in Saros…

'Baba said he would talk to her. She knows I'm not afraid of leaving. I've left before. If we both leave it would be impossible for them to run this place alone.'

'She said there were lots of girls on the island who would be eager to waitress here.'

'She said that! Ha!' He helped her to her feet, his arm around her waist, until she was sitting by the table against the counter, in Argyro's seat. 'While I was away, Dimitri told me, she went through every person who was available for work on the island. One after another they came and then left. First she employed her relatives, her cousins, but Dimitri said they did not hold back – after a day or so they each told her straight out that her attitude was unacceptable, they were not about to be talked to in the way she talked to them, and they left. Then she offered the position to youngsters who had just left school. Apparently she went through three of them, but each one never returned after the first day. I don't know what she expected on an island this small but, when she finally offered the work to anyone who wanted it, the word had got around. Baba said that, just before I came back, for a week they had no help and night after night they were trying to work out what to do until they thought of having you come over. Apparently they had had a notice up in the window for weeks offering the job but there was no one left on the island who would work with them. You cannot hide on an island. Everyone knows what she's like.'

'But now that you are back they really don't need me!' Vasso exclaimed. 'I mean, when they arranged for me to come, you were still away…'

'They need you, Vasso, because if you go, I go, and then they are stuck.'

'You make it sound like we're in a strong position.' Vasso managed a smile. Spiros stroked her hair.

'Yes, I suppose it does.' He managed to look a little brighter, but not much.

Stamatis came back after a while, and behind him Argyro, all anger wiped from her face. She walked like she was ready to fight, her arms out to the sides, each leg rolling around the other, but her face said something else. Vasso got up quickly from her seat and the dizziness returned. Spiros pulled her back down.

'I may have overstepped the mark,' Argyro muttered through clenched teeth.

'And?' Stamatis prompted.

'And congratulations.'

And she picked up her cigarettes, turned around and walked out.

When the day was at its hottest, Stamatis readied himself to leave for his afternoon sleep as usual.

'We'll see you at five,' he called, and looked first at Vasso, then Spiros, and winked. 'And not a moment before.'

The next two weeks passed without incident. Argyro spent less time in the taverna and Spiro's lunchtime service continued to be popular. Each night, under the lemon tree, they counted their drachmas and calculated how close they were to renting their own taverna. If they managed to keep going in the same way for the rest of the summer they wouldn't need Vasso's dowry, which could be used on a house instead. But they agreed that they should, very quietly, start asking around to see what was available and how much the rent would be. It wouldn't have to be by the port, which would be expensive. Anywhere would do. They both felt sure that people would come. Spiros said he had his eye on a place a few streets back from the port that had closed some years before. It had never been cleared out and still had its fridges and cookers.

'Shall I ask the owner if we can go and look around one night after we're closed here?' he said, and Vasso squeezed his hand and kissed him.

A letter arrived from Vasso's mama thanking her daughter for writing and congratulating her on her news. In the letter she chatted about which villagers she had told the good news to and how they had responded. Everyone was so delighted, she said. She fussed over the size of the trunk she had been preparing for years for this happy event. Her worry was that she had not managed to gather enough sheets yet, and there was a pillowcase that she had started to embroider years ago, ready for this day, but somehow it had been put back in the trunk unfinished. Would Vasso like her to come over sooner so they could arrange everything together, and where did she plan to honeymoon? The enthusiasm in her words reduced Vasso to tears and made her yearn to be back home. But Spiros dried her eyes, kissed her lips, engulfed her body and took her to places where she could think of nothing but him.

Shortly after this time, Argyro came in one morning and made it quite clear that something was on her mind.

'Spiro,' she called out to where he was serving coffee to a pair of tourists. Vasso headed outside to take his place. 'And you,' Argyro added, somewhat ungraciously.

'I'm not stupid,' she began, her voice low and controlled as if she had practised what she was going to say. Stamatis stopped rattling the pans and came out from behind the counter and stood by his son. Argyro's eyes narrowed but she made no comment. 'There are too many people on this island with wagging tongues for me not to know what is going on. Stamatis may be blind but I am not.'

'I have no idea what you are-' Spiros began but she silenced him with the flat of her hand in front of his face. To Vasso, this was *mountza*, an insult, and she bristled. Spiro's mouth became a thin line and the hand lowered.

'I have not found any food missing. If it was, and it was not paid for, that would be theft.' Her voice remained low. Vasso stared at her shoes.

'Argyro, what are you saying?' Stamati's face held all the disgust he managed to keep out of his voice.

'But what I think is going on is that you are using these premises – my premises – for your own gain without paying any rent.'

No one spoke. Vasso silently acknowledged that, technically, what she was saying was true.

'From the rumours, I hear you have done well, and, as I said, I am not stupid. If it were me I would be gathering my little pile of drachmas and thinking of getting my own place.'

Spiros drew a quick breath.

'What? You thought I wouldn't know? When you have been asking around for premises…?'

Spiros looked at Vasso and Vasso looked to see how this was affecting Stamatis. His eyebrows had risen in the middle and, even though he was a middle-aged man, he looked like he might cry.

'Look at you all, panicking,' Argyro scoffed. 'I am neither stupid, nor am I

139

unreasonable,' she went on. 'So I have an offer to make you. Stamatis, you can be waiter, Spiros you can be cook, but no one is going anywhere, you stay and you work here. I want your word on that.'

Vasso saw the relief across Stamati's face.

The three of them, ignoring Argyro, looked at each other, trying to gauge one another's reactions to the suggestion.

Eventually, Spiros looked at the floor and Vasso remembered him telling her how he had learnt to crawl there. Stamati's mouth hung open, his arms limp by his side, his eyes sad, resigned, awaiting the outcome. The seconds ticked by until Vasso took Spiro's hand. This would mean no more saving, no more of the stress of going behind Argyro's back, no more waiting for Spiros to take his rightful place in a kitchen. She gave his hand a squeeze.

'Agreed,' he said, and everyone, except him, sighed out their tension. 'But I get free rein on the menu.'

Argyro didn't answer; she gave a quick jerk of her chin, sideways and down in agreement.

But all Vasso could remember thinking at the time was that this tentative peace would not last.

Chapter 17

'You know, I've been here over a month now and I've seen nothing of the island,' Vasso reflected one night as they sat under the lemon tree.

'If Argyro does not buy better produce we are going to lose our customers,' Spiros mused. 'There's not much to see, it's an island after all…' He took a long drink of his third ouzo. 'The meat is too tough. You know, they do not hang meat here, in Greece. Meat needs to be hung so the natural enzymes can break down the meat, improve its flavour and make it tender. But the meat is too fresh. Butchered the same day as you buy it. It sounds great, but it makes it tough and flavourless. It won't do.'

'Do you think Argyro will let us have an afternoon off every other week or something, so I can explore the island?'

'We cannot hang it ourselves. The butcher told me it has to be done at a constant temperature. He'll do it for us, but he would charge more, of course. I've tried to explain this to Argyro, that I am compensating for the toughness and lack of flavour by cooking it for longer, more slowly, but she is saying it's just a waste of gas.'

'I'd like to walk up to the monastery, up at the top, on the ridge. Have you been up there? I bet the views are amazing...'

'And the vegetables! Can she not see they are not the best quality? I tell you this is going to ruin my reputation.'

'Spiro, are you listening to me?'

'Sorry, what?'

'I want us to have the odd afternoon off to see the island, or just to be together.'

'Ah Vasso, my baby. In an ideal world, eh?

'What do you mean, in an ideal world? It's not unreasonable.'

'No, I didn't say it was, but now we are running the taverna we have to be here for the customers.'

'Argyro is still running the taverna. She orders the produce, she pays the bills.'

'Ah, but she does not cook. I do!'

'Yes, and I'm very pleased for you, but maybe we need a little time too, Spiro.'

The leaves on the lemon tree rustled with the breeze. Spiros put down his glass, took her face in his hands and looked into her eyes. She

143

looked back into his, liquid pools of brown that promised so much.

'We have all winter, and the rest of our lives too,' he said and the kiss made her forget, and the night slid by and the morning came too soon.

'Green beans, beetroot, tomatoes, onions.' The donkey man with the sandy hair named each item as he dumped it on the doorstep.

'What are these?' Spiros picked up a long, pale, wilted bean.

'Beans,' the man answered, shrugging.

'Argyro, these will be stringy and tough,' he said, holding a handful of the offending beans under her nose. Argyro looked up briefly from her magazine and shrugged.

'Five drachmas less a kilo,' she said, and continued to read.

'No, it's not good enough. Stefanos,' He addressed the donkey man. 'Take it back.'

'I get paid to deliver,' said the man.

'Okay, I will pay you to take it back. Spiros was almost shouting as he stepped towards the till. Argyro was on her feet, magazine forgotten.

'And what do you think you are doing?' She stood between him and the till.

'If we keep getting this produce I will lose my reputation.'

'Your reputation! This is a taverna, not a one-man show!' Argyro snapped back.

'And the meat, it isn't fresh!'

'You said you wanted it old.'

'No, I wanted it hung. That's different from being old – it's controlled.'

'Stefanos, thank you.' Argyro said to the donkey man, who seemed relieved to be dismissed.

Vasso did not want to witness another row between Spiros and Argyro, so she watched Stefanos feed his donkey a handful of the wilted beans. The animal took them, its lips curling around the beans but avoiding his fingers, its muzzle soft against his calloused palm. Stefanos leaned in and whispered in its fluffy ear before untying the beast and moving off. There was something old about him, even though he was still in his twenties or thereabouts.

The voices inside the taverna were raised.

'If we do not cook this meat longer we will end up giving someone food poisoning.' Spiros was almost shouting.

'Keep your voice down,' Argyro hissed. Stamatis looked to Vasso. He appeared beaten and his stoop seemed more exaggerated as he wandered back out to the sunshine.

'You know, it's a Tuesday morning. There'll be no business until this afternoon. Take him out, Vasso, go for a walk by the sea. I'm sick of hearing them argue.'

'Really? Will you manage?'

'What? A frappé or two and flipping the lid off a cold beer! I think so.' But his humour didn't reach his eyes. 'Spiro,' he called inside.

The argument between Spiros and Argyro continued for a moment, and then Spiros came to join them.

'Spiro, take Vasso for a walk,' Stamatis said.

Vasso expected Spiros to object but instead he walked out into the sunshine and grabbed her hand, and they walked off along the harbour wall without a word.

She waited for a barrage of accusation to be voiced over Argyro's attitude, but he managed to walk silently. Was this a time to say silent, or should she try to smooth things over?

They walked on, around the far side of the port. The buildings on the harbour front had been built as warehouses, originally, with large doors to let the fishing boats in, but most had been converted some time ago and were now boutique shops, selling clothes and jewellery, reflecting the wealth of the tourists who came here.

It was an island where the rich and famous had their hideaways. Names were always popping up in the chatter amongst the customers, but she had no real idea if it was just gossip or true. An American musician was said to have had a house somewhere up in the town, and so did a very popular English actress who made Hollywood films.

'I have heard that a lot of rich and famous people from around the world live here.' She did not phrase it as a question. There was also a famous Greek painter who spent half the year amongst the locals. Vasso had seen one or two of his paintings, but could not understand why people liked them.

'And that Greek painter,' she added quietly.

Their pace was not slow and he still had a grip on her hand, so she hurried to keep up. The speed did not really feel conducive to conversation so she gave up trying and stayed quiet. It felt like he was taking her somewhere. Part of her wanted to pull away and suggest that he walk with her, not lead her like a goat. But her heart told her to let it be, to trust him, follow him, to remain as supportive as she could. She decided she would put up with being towed for another five minutes, but no longer than that.

Beyond the last of the shops, where the sea wall jutted out, enclosing the harbour, the land behind sloped up steeply, looming over the port. Vasso had not ventured this way until now, and she assumed that the path ended here, but as they approached the corner she could see that it curled round and followed the coast of the island, disappearing into inlets, reappearing further along, stretching along the island's coast as far as she could see. To her right there was a sound of screeching and laughter. With a hand against her forehead for shade she searched amongst the rocks for the shapes of people. Their arms swinging, and with mock severity, young boys pushed one another screaming off the rocks and into the depths, only to bob to the surface to laugh and call each other names. Looking out across the sea, she could see the sun reflecting from the surface so sharply she narrowed her eyes; the expanse of it took her breath away. Floating far, far away was the blue outline of the mainland, and in-between were dotted barren misty blue islands, on white lines of surf, offering a sense of distance. The nearest boasted a tiny whitewashed church.

'Oh, how beautiful,' Vasso said.

But Spiros did not reply, and he led her up a very steep set of steps. Up and up they went, Vasso growing ever hotter until her forearms shone with sweat and she thought she might have to ask Spiros to stop so she could rest.

But Spiros clearly did not want to talk and he did not want to stop, so she continued, their joined arms stretched out between them as he marched forward.

When there was nowhere higher to climb to, he dodged between two pine trees and down behind a wall. They passed a small church that looked like it had not been used for some time, and then they came out onto a terrace that surrounded an old windmill. The sails had gone and the door was propped shut with a stone. Half the terrace was in shade and here Spiros flopped onto the ground and sat cross-legged. Before them, the panorama of the sea was even broader, and the blue of the water and the blue of the sky were only separated by a thin line of darker blues that suggested land. Around the base of each island, a haze of white made it appear to levitate. Vasso was sure she had never seen a more breathtaking view in her life.

Chapter 18

'Oh, for the love of all that is good look at the view!' she exclaimed.

Spiros looked, but his attention was not on the view.

'She's got to go,' he said.

'Can we not forget about the taverna for now and just be together?'

'Okay, my love. But I am just letting you know that I have made a decision. The taverna was ours, my mama's, my baba's and mine, before she came along, so to make this work – which it is, but it will work even better – she has got to go.'

'I agree it would be easier.'

'Whatever it takes.' He spoke in a snarl, and Vasso looked at him; for the first time, she felt as if she did not know him. His intensity scared her.

And then he laughed. His laughter was young and carefree and it lit up his face.

'This is where I would come when I was a boy on my way home from school. I would take the long way.' He pointed over his shoulder, behind the hill to the next rise towards the ridge that ran like a spine along the whole island. There, a solid square building sat, with large letters painted on the side announcing to the world that it was the high school.

'Were you good at school?' Vasso asked, relieved at the change in subject.

'No, not really. The teachers liked me because I was always polite and on time but I had no ambition to do well. What for? If I could read, write and add up that was all I needed. I never had any intention of leaving the island. I loved my mama.' His voice turned sad. 'I was happy just to be with her, her and Baba.'

Vasso knew it was only her curiosity that made her want to ask how his mama had died, and it was a subject that would not cheer Spiros, so she stayed silent.

'Dimitri, he was naughty. Oh, how he was naughty.' Spiros rolled back on his hips as he laughed. 'He was naughty enough for the both of us. I would find him up here quite often, hiding from whatever trouble he was in.'

Vasso delighted in this recollection. Staring out to sea, she could imagine them both there, two boys, one good and one naughty, each wishing just a little to be more like the other, each also glad that he wasn't.

A noise caught her attention, and she peered over the edge of the terrace and down the steep slope that dropped to the path and then to the sea below them. A little way down, on an impossibly narrow ledge, was a goat.

'Nee, nee.' She wobbled her throat in imitation of the animal. It looked up and answered, the bell around its neck clonking a dull resonance. 'Look, it's coming to us – oh, its feet are tied!' A length of rope was strung between a front and a back leg.

'Keeps it safe,' Spiros said. 'Stops them being too adventurous, jumping about. They've been known to fall in the sea.'

'Really?'

'They say.'

'So, have you never wanted to leave the island, then, not even when you got to be about – I don't know, fourteen or fifteen, and home seemed too small?' She could remember that feeling, of her own village seeming to be too small, everyone knowing everyone else's business – imagining their eyes watching her wherever she went. At thirteen it had been excruciating, and at fourteen she had wanted to run away just to give them all something to talk about. Her friend, Stella, had become fidgety at that age, too. In fact, their friendship had faltered for a while, each had become so agitated. Poor Stella did not get on too well with her own mama, and at that time she had even begun to argue with her baba, whom previously it had seemed she adored. For Vasso, going home was a sanctuary from the people of the village, whereas Stella complained that it felt like the village but more concentrated, with two against one in a small house. With a less sensitive man than Stella's baba, that could have been a very uncomfortable time for her friend, but, true to his character, he found a way to reach his daughter, provided the safety she needed, and very quickly became Stella's idol again.

'Never.' Spiros was emphatic. 'I wanted to cook in the taverna. That was it. That's always been it and now I'm absolutely determined that will be it!' He spoke angrily again.

Vasso twisted her engagement ring and sighed.

'Spiro, where will we live?'

'Hmmm?'

'After we are married. Will we live at your family home?'

'What? With Argyro?'

'Well, we have to live somewhere.'

'I haven't given it any thought.' He seemed far away. Maybe he was tired.

'Perhaps we should? Also – when shall we marry?'

'I think I will do pork for the special tonight.'

'Spiro!'

'I'm kidding. What about at the end of the summer?'

'Here, or in my village?'

'Here, of course. I think I *will* do the pork though, with celery, dill and *avgolemono* sauce.'

'I don't have so much family, so from my side it will be a small wedding. Who is there on your side?'

'Who *isn't* there on my side? The whole island is related to each other if you go far enough back.'

'Well, we can use what we kept back from the lunchtime service before Argyro found us out... I'm afraid there won't be much money from Mama, because that's why I'm here. So we can't afford to invite them all.'

'It will work out. Don't worry, my sweet. Come here.' His face was close to hers. 'I never imagined *you* when I was up here as a boy.' He wrapped her hair around his fist and ever so gently pulled her towards him. 'If I had I would have been the most impatient boy in the world, waiting for you.' He kissed her nose, her eyes, her cheeks, her mouth, and the view and the windmill no longer existed. There was only Spiros. They remained interlocked for several minutes until Spiros pulled away and said, 'Come on. If it is to be pork I need to get started.' And he was on his feet, pulling her up by her hand, pausing for another kiss, and then they were laughing and chasing each other as they headed back to the taverna. The world was a beautiful place.

'You took your time,' Argyro greeted them.

'Pork tonight!' Spiros said as he bounced behind the counter.

'Well, don't have it cooking all afternoon, it's a waste of gas.'

A brief frown from Spiros and a tightening of his jaw told Vasso that his good mood was already gone. Maybe she could help?

'Perhaps it needs cooking for that long,' she ventured.

'Oh, so now we have two cooks. That's all we need.' And with this she indicated a pile of dirty cups in the sink.

Vasso sighed and started on the washing-up.

Needless to say, a few hours later there was an argument about the length of time the pork had been in the oven. It reached the point where Argyro was turning it off and Spiros was turning it on again. If it hadn't been so sad it would have been comical. Vasso kept one eye on the open door, hoping that Stamatis was unaware, but voices were now raised and customers who were about to sit walked away.

The pork was delicious, however. Since she had been eating Spiro's cooking, Vasso had put on weight. Not much, but she was pleased that she was not quite the stick that she had been when she first arrived. She almost had curves.

Spiros did not stay around the taverna that night. He said he was exhausted and left very soon after Stamatis and Argyro. It was strange being in the courtyard and then in her little room by herself, and a little lonely.

That night, she dreamt of pigs eating celery, their little tails wagging with joy, and when she woke she lurched to the bathroom and was violently sick.

Chapter 19

'You're up late.' Stamatis was brushing the leaves from the courtyard. Vasso did not dare speak. There was nothing left in her stomach but she still felt she might be sick again. 'You don't look too well. Are you alright?'

Managing a 'yes, thanks', she went through to the taverna, unsure how to handle the situation. It felt like food poisoning – a disaster for a taverna. Should she tell Argyro what she suspected – that it was the result of her short cooking times? Or should she broach the subject with Spiros, knowing it would result in more arguing between the pair?

'You ill?' Argyro glanced up from her magazine, coffee in one hand, cigarette in the other. The smell of the cigarette turned Vasso's stomach.

'Oh, you alright?' Spiros came around from the counter and led her to the front door, towards the fresh air.

'Always something with that one, sickly little thing,' Argyro grumbled, and she continued to read her paper.

'Spiro.' Vasso sat at one of the tables, all of which were empty this early in the morning. 'I think that perhaps you were right about the cooking times.' He looked at her quizzically. 'I think I may have food poisoning. I've just been really sick.'

First he turned white and then a deep red flush rose from his neck, up into his cheeks. He pulled his arms back from around her and put his hands flat on the table, but as her words sank in he clenched his fists, the knuckles turning white. He pushed himself up from the table.

'Please, Spiro. Please don't argue with her today. I cannot stand it any more.' She didn't expect him to do her bidding but as he looked into her face he sat down again.

'But this could be a disaster. If everyone who ate the pork last night gets sick that will be that. No one will come again, and we will have to close.' He looked across the harbour. The yachts, sporting flags from around the world, were moored side by side, some two or three deep off the pier. They bobbed gently and the halyards clicked lightly against the masts. The sun reflected off the sea beyond the harbour wall. So peaceful, but for Vasso just the sight of the water moving made her head swim, and she feared she might be sick again.

'We must talk with Stamatis and Argyro.' He stood decisively and beckoned his baba, who was talking to Ilias the fisherman down by the water's edge. They were discussing the morning catch.

'Please do not argue,' Vasso implored as they headed into the taverna, Stamatis following.

Inside, Argyro looked up from her magazine and sighed.

'Now what?' she asked.

'We have a problem.' Spiros kept his tone steady.

'Don't I know it!' Argyro muttered and looked back to her magazine.

'Vasso got food poisoning from last night's pork.'

Vasso expected him to add, 'because you would not let me cook it long enough.' She waited; they all waited, but he said no more.

Both Argyro and Stamatis stared at her.

'I was really sick,' Vasso said, and wondered why she felt guilty.

'I had the pork,' Argyro said. 'And I feel fine.' One side of her upper lip curled up at Vasso. 'Stamatis, you had it too, didn't you?' But there was an edge of anxiety in her voice.

'I did, I did.' Stamatis eagerly placated her.

'Well, then?' Argyro waited for Spiros to say something.

'So maybe it was not all of the pork, just some of it – the trays that were cooked nearer the bottom of the oven perhaps, where it was cooler? It will only take one or two people to be sick to kill my business.'

'Our business,' Argyro corrected and Vasso felt like she was losing the ability to remain standing. But she was not going to give Argyro the satisfaction of seeing her collapse again, no matter how weak she felt.

'Did you notice who else I served from the same *tapsi*?' Spiros asked her.

'Dimitri,' Vasso answered.

'So if he is sick then we have trouble.'

Stamatis was already out of the taverna and turning towards Dimitri's little shop, where he sold miniature plaster windmills with the word *Orino* written on the sails, ashtrays with dolphins across the bottom and the words *Orino Island* around the edge, and other tourist paraphernalia.

The others waited in silence, watching the doorway, the islanders walking past, a boat coming into harbour. Argyro did not even care that a group of backpackers had sat down outside and no one had rushed out to serve them.

Stamatis came back smiling. 'He's fine,' and all eyes turned on Vasso.

'I *was* sick!' she protested.

Argyro sighed heavily, as if the weight of the world was on her shoulders and nothing could be done about it. She pointed out the tourists to Stamatis and returned to her magazine.

'Vasso, will you be alright? I need to start on the lunchtime food,' Spiros said as he went behind the counter, and then he was lost to her, in his world of cooking. After a few minutes he spoke to Argyro.

'How did you like that scare? Better not to risk it, wouldn't you say?' and Argyro made the smallest movement, blinking and shifting her chin sideways and down, in very subtle agreement.

Vasso remained standing exactly where the whole discussion had started, with no one near her. Spiros was lost in preparation, Stamatis was busy chatting to the German backpackers, suggesting a cold glass of beer, and her own mama was across the water, so far away.

Her stomach had stopped complaining but now she felt like crying. She wanted to go home.

161

Looking over to Spiros, even his beauty did not seem enough to make her want to stay. She twisted the ring on her finger and wondered how she had managed to become entangled in this feuding family. The thought crept up on her that maybe she was nothing but a distraction for Spiros, because, now that he was cooking, he seemed to have precious little time for her, ring or no ring.

Maybe she *had* been foolish to get engaged so soon. But it had all felt so right – so overpoweringly right.

It occurred to her, however, that perhaps it was Argyro who was right, and that she had indeed been rash in accepting Spiro's advances so soon, and she found herself wondering whether she had given everything to a man who perhaps, maybe, did not even care about her. But no...! Could it really be wrong? She tried to push these thoughts away.

There it was again – the sensation that the world was spinning, the precursor to fainting. No way was she going to give in. Blinking hard, she marched on stiff legs to the courtyard, into her room and through it to swill her face with cold water in the sink. The spinning receded, but she still felt like crying.

With a wet face, she sat on the edge of the neatly made bed. For so many nights this bed had been a place of such harmony and comfort, but recently it had seemed to offer loneliness and longing. So much had happened so quickly. How long had she even been here, now? She had arrived... Now, when had it been? The days had merged one into another. The corners of the printed icon above her bed had curled in the heat, and the whole thing was kept straight only by the weight of the calendar stuck on its bottom edge. The curled leaf said it was July, but perhaps it was already August and she had forgotten to tear off the page. She tried to work out the days, make sense of the time – and then the blood rushed in her ears and her forehead turned to ice – the reason she was sick loomed with such force that her hands began to shake, and the rest of her turned to stone. Last week should have been her uncomfortable week, but it had passed unnoticed.

She was pregnant!

Chapter 20

How on earth had such a thing happened? At first she had been nervous, and he had reassured her again and again. He said he was being so careful. And he *was* being careful. Even on those later occasions when she was ready to throw caution to the wind he had been steadfast. So how could it happen? An accident, a slim chance? Why had she thought she was immune to such an event? Because it felt so right? Because they were engaged? What on earth had possessed her to take any risk at all, no matter how remote? But she knew the answer to that, too. She had allowed the risk because Spiros possessed her. He had noticed her, made her real, made her feel beautiful, desirable. Someone as handsome as Spiros had lifted her out of her own perception of herself and made her feel that she was so much more than she really was!

But what she had actually become was less. Now she was a stupid young girl, pregnant out of wedlock.

She checked the calendar again. Maybe she was wrong, had miscalculated. But the brief hope was extinguished before it took a firm hold.

Back in her village, everyone knew what sort of girl got pregnant before marriage. She had known from quite a young age. Her own mama was always quick to tell people when they first met that her husband had died – an explanation for Vasso's existence, in case her faded widow's weeds were not enough to bestow respectability.

And yet here was Vasso, a decent woman, daughter of a decent woman, unmarried and pregnant. And, therefore, no longer respectable.

Her head dropped into her hands and the tears that had been threatening all morning burst from her in big wailing sobs. She held her hand over her mouth but the truth was she did not care who heard. Wailing and crying were so much less a public offence than her real crime.

'Oh God in heaven, have mercy on me,' she called, but in that moment she felt there was no God. If there was and he was fair he would not have allowed her to become pregnant. If there was a God, he had deserted her – and maybe she deserved that. No maybe about it! Had she not been taught that it was not God's law?

She wailed anew and sank to her knees.

'Please, please, God, let this not be true. Let me be wrong. Let this not be happening. Please find a way to take this away.' And a dreadful thought came to her that was surely even worse than an unmarried pregnancy. Was there a way? Would it be such a sin, so early on?

She shook her head and the tears did not stop. She might be the sort of person who could become pregnant before she was married, but she would not become a murderer – because, according to what the Church had taught her, that was what it would be. 'Isn't it?' she asked out loud, because somewhere in the back of her mind she could remember hearing of a woman who had done just that – a woman who was married to a man who beat her and who did not want to risk having children. Or was all that just gossip?

'What are you doing on the floor?' Stamatis asked, peering into her room.

She flinched, not having expected anyone to come, no matter how hard she sobbed. But why could it not have been Spiros? If it had been Spiros he could have taken her in his arms and made it alright, couldn't he?

'Are you still sick?' Stamatis helped her up onto the bed.

'I was trying to pray,' Vasso sobbed.

'Oh, sorry, am I interrupting?

'No – please don't go.'

'I'm sorry you are unwell – can I get you anything?'

'No.' She waited, weighing it all up and wondering what to do. 'Stamati,' she began, after a pause.

'Yes – what is it, little one?' His tone tender.

'I want to tell you something.'

'Then tell me.' His voice was soft.

'It's not easy.'

'Then tell me slowly.'

She remained silent.

'Or tell me all of a rush and get it out quickly.' Stamatis chuckled at his own joke.

'I think that, if Spiros is serious, we need to get married sooner rather than later.'

Stamatis said nothing, but she could almost hear his mind working. After a minute or two a new light came to his eyes as he made the connection.

'You mean?' He looked from her face to her stomach.

Vasso nodded.

'Fantastic!' Stamatis was grinning from ear to ear. 'Oh, congratulations, my dear.' And he took her into a hug so tight she could feel all the bones of his ribcage against hers. When he released her, he was still smiling, but she wasn't. It was a relief that Stamatis had reacted in such a way, of course, but how would Spiros respond?

'Does Spiros know?' Stamatis asked, when he saw that she still looked sad.

'No. I'm not sure he will be pleased. He's all absorbed in his cooking.'

'He will be delighted!' Stamatis replied – a little too quickly. 'Shall I bring him in so you can tell him?'

Now, later – did it really matter when?

'Erm… before I call him' – Stamatis faltered – 'um, well, it does occur to me that, well, to be – it's, well, um, Argyro…' Little beads of sweat formed on his forehead as he struggled to express himself. 'She has this way of relating things to herself. I mean, I don't want to take the joy out of this but it is possible that she might not be as pleased as I am, because – well, because she cannot have children, do you see?'

'You are a good man, Stamati,' Vasso said, after listening to him struggle to tell her what she probably could have worked out for herself, had she thought about it.

168

'I will get Spiros.' He patted her hand and stood. 'Spiro, can you come here?'

'Not just at the moment... I'm just sealing the chicken,' came the reply.'

'If you can, it is rather important.' Stamatis gave Vasso a smile and then left, meeting Spiros in the courtyard. She heard a brief muttered exchange as they passed each other, and then Spiro's head appeared around the doorway.

'Are you feeling any better?' he asked, and looked back to his kitchen. 'What is so important?' His fingers fidgeted on the doorpost.

'Spiro, I need to know you love me.'

'Of course I love you. Have I not told you I love you? And you have a ring on your finger. Can we not have this talk when I'm not cooking? It's just that the chicken...'

Vasso looked down at her hands. 'I'm pregnant,' she said quietly.

His fingers stopped moving. His eyes widened. Was that a look of joy or horror? She could not tell. He seemed to remain immobile for minutes, longer, but a part of Vasso knew it could only be seconds.

'That's great,' he said finally, but he was still by the doorpost and his voice was not strong, it was not sure. Then he moved, he was in the room, he sat next to her, took her in his arms, kissed her hair, put her head under his chin. 'That's fantastic.' Now he sounded sincere.

'Really?' she asked.

'Really.' He held her even tighter.

'I cannot tell my mama. Not till we are married.' She pulled away so she could look at him.

'Then we must get married as soon as we can. I will make *kokkinisto*. If we invite one person from Orino we will have to invite them all. That will be – well, it could be up to a thousand people passing by, more even. We will need five hundred kilos of meat. I must talk to Stefano's baba. You know, Stefanos the donkey boy? He has a big goat herd. The tomatoes – if we need to, we can ship them from the mainland...'

'Spiro!' Argyro's harsh tones came from the taverna.

'I can borrow larger pans from one of the hotels…'

'Spiro!'

'Yes, yes, it will be amazing.'

'Spiro!'

'And I will need some smoked paprika!'

'Spiro!' Argyro yelled again. 'Something is burning.'

'Coming!' He was on his feet and was about to leave when he paused to take Vasso's

170

face in both hands and kiss her, then left with a real spring to his step. But Vasso wondered whether the life in his limbs was because of the child in her belly or the thought of cooking for the whole of the island.

After quickly tidying her hair, she left the courtyard through the side gate.

Chapter 21

The side street was a dead end if she went inland, and the other way it led to the harbour. She pressed herself to the wall and peeped round to see what Stamatis was doing, which way he was facing. He was assisting a very pale-skinned woman, who was wearing shorts and a big floppy hat, her finger tracing down the menu that Stamatis held for her.

Looking the other way, Vasso judged that she could dodge between people, nip behind a laden donkey and make her way unseen. Stamatis probably wouldn't notice her at all if she walked at a steady pace.

The only part of the island she knew was the harbour, and the coastal path that led from it. She released her hair from its ponytail and pulled it across to half cover her face. When Stamati's customer sat down and he went trotting inside with her order, Vasso set off, first very briskly to cover maximum distance, and later slowing down so as not to attract attention. Where the last shop gave way to the rock face she allowed herself to relax a little, and, as she did so, tears welled onto her lower lids and she tried to blink them away. The sun on the water was almost blinding to her blurred eyes, and she stumbled on, not knowing where she was going or even why. She just wanted to go, put distance between herself and Spiros, be far away from the smells of cooking and the bickering and Argyro. Really, she knew she wanted to go home but she also knew she could not – not as long as she was single. Her mama would die of shame. Most likely, her mama would send her back and tell her not to return until she was married. That was just how things were.

Further along, where the path turned inland behind a rock, a shape appeared. A man and a donkey. She did not want to see anyone. Her eyes were sure to be puffy and she could not pretend to be anything other than miserable, but there was no avoiding the meeting and she walked on. The figure grew closer and with a sudden spark she recognised Stefanos – from the way he moved, more than anything else.

She could not face seeing him. There was something wise and far-seeing about the man, as if he only saw people on a deep level. That was the last thing she needed. She ducked under a tree to her left and, after climbing a little, she

173

found the steps Spiros had taken her up the day they had gone to the windmill.

But today she did not walk so fast and she stopped before she reached the top, turning around to admire the view and take a little rest. There was no sign of Stefanos on the path below and she wondered where he had gone.

Once she recovered her breath, she pushed on until she reached the top. The effort of it all kept her thoughts at bay, for which she was grateful, but after she passed the little church and emerged by the old windmill her scrambled emotions all returned, crowding in on her, each more pressing than the last.

'You look troubled,' came a quiet voice.

Vasso nearly jumped out of her skin. Peering in amongst the pine trees down the steep slope she made out the donkey first, munching away at the base of one of the trees, seeking out little patches of green that were defying the parched days of summer.

'I think there's a bit of run-off here or something,' Stefanos said, pointing at the weeds his donkey was eating. 'They do go brown and shrivel, but it takes another week just here. They are already dead everywhere else on the island. She loves them.' He patted his donkey's neck, released the rein and left the animal to eat as he climbed the last few steps to the windmill's base.

'So, why the sad look?' He sat down facing the sea, turning his head slowly as he took in the whole view.

'Nothing.' Vasso did not want to talk about it. Not to him, not to Spiros, not to anybody.

'Yes, I know that nothing,' he said. 'Is it possible to live a life and not have your heart broken?' It seemed a strange comment from someone who appeared so content. 'My wife lost our first child this time last year. Now I wait for my second to be born. My mother thinks it will be a boy. She is a midwife, so she should know. If it is a boy, we will call him Yianni and he too will be a donkey man.' Stefanos sounded proud. 'But for now I wait and I hope, and sometimes I even pray. But it is easy to stop praying when you lose a child.'

It took her by surprise. Firstly, because he did not seem much older than her – but then why shouldn't someone their age have a child? Her hand crept over her stomach. And secondly, she had just not imagined him being married; he seemed so remote, so distant. She looked at the back of his head. His hair was matted, presumably from sleeping on it, and there was an aroma of goats about him. His clothes were far from new and his boots were scuffed and

175

worn. It was difficult to imagine him enjoying a love affair – yet he had a wife and a baby on the way. And there was something very attractive about his face, even though he was unshaven and his hair was unruly. When they had first talked, down at the port, she had noticed that his eyes had all the signs of real intelligence clicking away behind them. It was his outer layer she had trouble imagining anyone wanting to get close to.

'But I trust this time he will be born safe. Yanni, son of Stefanos. It is enough.'

'I wish you and your family well,' Vasso said. They sat in silence for a while. Stefanos was not much older than her, and he had already lost one child. Her perspective shifted as she digested this thought. The life growing inside her became real, a little person. A strange sensation crept across her chest, and as it spread it expanded – it drew in her heart, her mind, brought strength to her limbs, her whole being. It was a force that had no limits, a passion that had no boundaries. It was love, love for her unborn child, a jealous, protective, passionate love.

'I have a theory–' Stefanos began, but then stopped. Vasso waited. He continued to look out to sea for several minutes without speaking.

'Tell me your theory,' she said, but he didn't react, and she began to wonder if he had heard her. The sensation of her all-consuming love lingered, but there was more to it, now. In her mind arose the thought: 'I am no longer alone.' This struck Vasso as odd; she had never felt alone – or, at least, not completely. But this was different. This was a sense of not needing anyone else, of a developing toughness. A sense that she need rely on no one else to protect her baby. She, herself, would do whatever it took.

'I think people love,' Stefanos said. 'Or they think they love. They meet, fall in love, get married, have children. But then, if their partner does not continue to love them they think they have a broken heart – but do they? Is what they had really love, or is fulfilment of their parents' expectations and a brief courtship and marriage just the quickest route to the easy family life they think is theirs by right?' His words came out quickly and Vasso tried to process them as he continued. 'I think, only if you have loved and that person has been taken away, for whatever reason, do you really know the depth of your love, why you love them, how that person fulfils a part of you and makes you whole. Only then, when your heart so yearns for them, can you say it is truly broken.'

Vasso did not respond, unsure how to. His concepts seemed strange – reflective perhaps of his own experiences. Or maybe she would have these thoughts, too, if she spent as much time in deep reflection as it seemed Stefanos had.

The donkey's hooves clicked against the stones as it made its way towards its master.

'Those sound like very wise words,' she finally replied, feeling that she didn't understand all he had said and that she would have to think more deeply now she was responsible for the tiny heartbeat inside her.

'Just an observation,' he said as the donkey went round behind him, nudged him with its muzzle. Stefano's weather-beaten hand took the reins that dangled by his ear. 'So, is your heart really broken?' he asked.

'I never said it was.' She searched his face, hoping to find wisdom there, but what she saw was pain at the understanding that life could take away his loved ones. There was something else, though, or at least she imagined there was – a pragmatic acceptance, which she had previously mistaken for contentment.

'People cry either for love or money. You don't strike me as the type to cry for money.' He stood and stretched.

'So if I cry for love and my love has not gone away then my heart is not broken?' Vasso smiled at her question, not taking her own words very seriously, knowing she was simplifying what he had been saying. It was a relief to inject some levity into this rather serious conversation.

'Maybe you are crying because he is still there. That is another thing I have observed. People pretend to be in love because they are too scared to make a break.'

'Or they might be married.'

'You do not have to physically leave to make a break.'

'You are so deep!'

'But it's true, no?' He looked at the palm of his hand and then rubbed it down his trousers.

'Well, yes, I suppose so,' Vasso replied. Then he smiled at her and it was as if everything he said was wiped away and the world was full of joy.

'See you,' he said, and his donkey and the smell of goats headed with him up past the windmill towards the small church and the way she had come.

'Extraordinary,' she told the breeze, but somehow she felt a little lighter.

Chapter 22

She sat and watched the morning turn to afternoon, the shadows grow shorter. Across the expanse of water, fishing boats floated aimlessly, whilst others moved steadily, trailing lines through the calm sea, their ripples casting ever outwards until they flattened or hit the shore.

The intensity of the sun grew as it reached its height. Vasso mirrored its journey as she shuffled around the mill, staying in the shade. Down on the rippling blue glass the boats dispersed, the fishermen retreating in search of cool harbours. As the world became still and there was little to watch, her thoughts turned back to her predicament and what she should do.

It was then that she had the idea to try the mill door. It was a distraction and she knew it was, but maybe, if she did not think, by some miracle a solution would come to her. At worst, as time passed the reality of it would settle inside her and she would reach a place of acceptance rather than horror.

The stone against the door was a good size and it would not roll away with a push of her foot. As it was speckled with dried mud and goat droppings she did not want to use her hands. Looking around, she found an unused fence post, propped against a tree stump, as if left there for the purpose.

It levered the stone away from the door quite easily. The stone rolled over twice and the gap was wide enough for her to pass through.

Outside, the windmill was circular, so she was not sure why she found the roundness of the room a surprise. Maybe it was because every time she had been through a door she had been met with flat walls and square corners, or maybe it was because the few pieces of furniture that could fit in the place were at odd angles against the curve of the wall.

There was a wooden bed, crudely made, lashed across with rough brown rope. An aged yellow-brown, stripy mattress was folded up at one end. There was a small wardrobe, the door of which was missing and which looked like it might collapse at a touch. These two items gave the impression that no one had lived there for years. But on the sill of the single small, glassless window that looked out over the sea was an empty wine bottle with the stub of a candle, and another wine bottle lay on its side on the floor. Beside the second one were crisp pieces of dried orange peel. It could not have been very old as the remains still infused the room with a hint of orange essence.

Above were the wooden bones of the upper floor, the boards now missing, and, higher still, where the roof should have been, was half made of open sky.

The difference in temperature was enough to make her loiter, but after a minute or two and some gazing out of the window she could no longer feel the effects of the shade. Everywhere was hot at this time of year.

She sat on the hard edge of the bed. Since arriving on the island she had had little sleep. The mattress might have been grubby but the temptation to lie down and block out the world with dreams was more than she could resist. She flipped the mattress back to find a relatively clean sheet folded inside. Maybe someone was staying there, or perhaps they came, as she had, to rest in the heat of the day.

Shaking the sheet to dislodge any insects, she covered the mattress and lay down. Just lying still in the heat felt delicious. With her hand on her belly she concentrated to see if she could feel anything. A grumble reminded her she had not eaten. She concentrated harder. There was a small life in there, a tiny being who would fight to live like all other living things do. It might have no name and no personality now but it would still fight for its existence. Given life, it, too, would grow and one day have children of its own who would love it as she loved her own mama. Maybe she would become to it what her mama was to her. That was quite a thought. Maybe she would love it as her mama loved her. Why wouldn't she? And if that were the case, would she also have room in her heart for Spiros? Was it possible to love two people with such intensity? Then again, if she had such love for this child, would it really matter if Spiros spent all his time cooking? The child might be enough.

Ah, Spiros. Still so beautiful, but how quickly he had become so involved with his work that there was no time for anything else.

'Is that like all men?' she asked a seagull soaring high above the missing part of the roof.

Maybe this was the way of life. How would she know? She had never known her baba. She had never witnessed a marriage from inside a home. Maybe all courtships started with that flush of interest, only to level out to the practicality of everyday life. But so quickly?

And what of Stefano's thoughts? Did such pain as the loss of an unborn child give you insight?

Closing her eyes, she reflected that it would be very simple to let go, let herself drift, and why not? Did she not deserve to sleep now she was taking care of a little one?

Her hands slipped from her stomach as she allowed herself the luxury of oblivion.

It was the sound of munching that woke her. At first, she had no idea what it was, or where she was, but as she recalled her walk to the windmill she presumed that the munching came from Stefano's donkey, that he had come back. The sleep had creased her all over so she stretched and looked through the small window to the wide expanse of blue sea. She must have slept a long time as the hills of the mainland in the distance had taken on the purple hue of sunset. Pushing her head out, she looked down the steep bank towards the path and the sea, but below her she saw, not Stefano's donkey, but a herd of goats in amongst the scrubland, surrounding the mill.

The inside of the mill was now hotter than the cooling day outside so, leaving the mattress refolded, she carefully replaced the stone outside the door. The goats scattered at the sight of her, but then forgot she was there as they struggled to find enough to eat and closed around her again as if she were one of the herd.

There would be a shepherd somewhere, and she hoped she would not have to meet him. For the moment, it was enough to be alone.

One goat, its front hooves halfway up a tree trunk, stretched its neck as far as it could reach, and nibbled at the leaves on the lower branches. Its tongue curled from its mouth, hooking the thin twigs. She was so absorbed in watching that she did not hear someone approaching her from behind.

Chapter 23

'There you are! I've been worried sick.' Arms swooped around her and she recognised him by his musky scent as her face was held against his shirt. Spiro's grip was around her so fast, and was so tight, that the top of her ear got bent over, and it hurt.

'I've been all over the island looking for you,' he said, releasing her enough to look her in the face. As she rubbed at her ear she wanted to believe him, but the timing seemed just about right for him to have finished cooking for the evening customers. And why would he look for her anywhere else on the island, when this was the only place she knew?

'I panicked. I thought you might have gone back across.' He let her pull away a little more but he did not release her. The worried look in his eyes seemed genuine now. His mouth moved slowly towards her and he kissed her tenderly.

'Why did you leave?' he asked again as he rested his forehead on hers.

'You had to cook.'

'Well, yes. You know I have to cook, but why did you leave?' He pulled her into him again, her face in his hair this time, which smelt faintly of chicken and rosemary.

'Because you don't really need a baby in your life and I am beginning to wonder if you even need a wife,' she said gently in his ear.

'I think those hormones that you are supposed to get when you're pregnant must be kicking in already.' He released her a little, to hold her by her shoulders. 'Seriously, though – please don't ever disappear again. Tell me if you need space. I will understand.'

She allowed some of her fears to subside and she wondered if she had in fact overreacted.

'It just seems to me that now is a bad time to be having a baby, just as you are getting going, establishing your place on the island. I mean, you still have to depend on Argyro for ordering the food, and nothing is really settled. I should think the last thing you need to think about is a little life that is dependent on you.'

'Ah, well, there you are wrong.' He sounded triumphant.

She looked at him. How could he be so sure?

'We don't even know how Argyro is going to take the news. She might–' Vasso began.

'She's fine. In fact she is more than fine,' Spiros was quick to tell her.

'How do you mean?' Vasso waited for a reply but Spiros just shrugged as if he didn't know what else to tell her. 'I'm not sure I trust her, Spiro. Even Stamatis thought she might take it badly. You know – get jealous because she can't have children.'

'Well, then, she has surprised us all! She is absolutely fine about it and she now says that you should not be living in that room at the back of the taverna. As my fiancée, you should have a place in the house with us. She's arranging for you to have the spare room until we are married.'

'Really?'

'Really.'

The relief she felt rushed over her and loosened all the muscular knots that she hadn't even realised she was trying to relax in her back and her neck. It felt like someone had poured cooling water over her head, and the aching in her temples was instantly gone.

'Really?' she asked again.

'Yes, really!' Spiros assured her.

'She isn't jealous or cross or anything?'

'Quite the opposite. She's happy for us.'

'It doesn't fit.' The calm sea was dotted again with silhouettes of small fishing boats, men out to relax after a day's work, trying for a fish for their supper.

'No, but I am not going to question it. Let's just enjoy!' Spiros replied.

'Do you trust her?'

'I don't understand. What is there not to trust? We are getting married, you are having our baby and she wants to be there for you!'

Vasso settled in next to him, his arm around her so they could watch the setting sun. After a couple of minutes' reflection, Vasso added, 'Spiro? It is one thing to be happy for us, and another thing to say she is "there for me". Did she really use those words?'

'No, she really did say she intended to be there for you and the baby.'

'What does that mean?'

'It means we can be happy.' He kissed her hair.

'Being there as in when I need her, or being there as in getting in the way like she does with your cooking?'

189

'I think you need to relax. It's fine. It's all going to be fine.'

The sun had turned orange now and grown bigger as it dipped its edge into the sea. The sky had turned pink and purple and yellow, the colours blurring one into another. The goats had wandered up past them and they could hear their little hooves clicking across the church courtyard, the bells clanging dully, responding to the call of the shepherd somewhere behind the mill.

'Besides, I think most girls would be happy to be offered help with a young one. To have someone on hand for when you get tired, or need a break.'

Vasso could see how that would be good.

'If Argyro was the one who got up in the night for the baby, for example, then you would not be too tired to be by my side during the day.'

Vasso stiffened.

'With her help we could have our cake and eat it, too, as they say.' He smiled as he talked.

'What do you mean?' Vasso sat up a little.

'Well, if you have help with the baby then there is really no need for it to interrupt what we are doing in the taverna. The business works well with you, me and Stamatis. If Argyro was away, and kept busy, it would work even better, perhaps?'

'Are you suggesting that we use our child to keep Argyro from the taverna?' Like bait, she thought, but did not say the word. She pulled out from under his arm.

'No, no, no, sit down, stop getting so excited. I was just mulling over how there are many ways we could move forward and that perhaps – no, not perhaps, I feel sure that with a child the whole situation will only be better. Come.' He held his arm out for her to nestle into him again.

'Anyway,' he said when she was safely next to him, 'Argyro did mention that perhaps I would like to take over the whole running of the taverna.'

'She did?' Vasso sat up straight again. 'At what cost?'

'At no cost, my love. She just said that if we were so busy we wanted her to look after the baby then perhaps we'd better take over the whole running of the taverna.'

Vasso broke free of his arm, forgot about the sun ready to sink beneath an oscillating horizon, and stood to face him.

'Can you hear yourself or are you deaf?'
Spiros looked shocked.

'She is saying that if she brings up the baby we can have the taverna! And you are even contemplating this?'

Chapter 24

It was hard to see the details of his face in the twilight but she could clearly make out his mouth hanging open, the look of shock in his eyes.

'I'm not saying that! Why would you even think that I would suggest such a thing?' He sounded hurt.

'Because that is what it sounds like and I know exactly how wrapped up in your cooking you are.' She held her ground, although everything in her wanted to smooth over her accusation, repair the hurt.

'Vasso, you do not know me.'

That hurt her in return and reminded her of just how short a time she had actually known him. There would be many a person, both on the island, she guessed, and definitely back in her village, who would tell her that she had not known him long enough. But it was too late to go back. There was a baby now and that must come first.

'So, when do we marry, Spiro?' The question caught him off guard and he hesitated.

'You see, you are not ready.'

Spiros stood. He was not much taller than her, but he seemed to tower over her and it was enough to silence her.

'Come.' He held out his hand. 'Well, come on then!' He lurched towards her, took a firm hold of her hand and pulled her up past the mill and back along the path, the way she had come. They passed the little church and the wall and then, instead of turning down the steps to the harbour, he strode right up to a little house that was hidden behind the wall, in amongst a clump of pine trees. The gate hung open and a dull light came from behind some shutters, but apart from that the place appeared to be sleeping. Spiros banged on the door with such authority that anyone within would think there was a fire, an emergency. But no one came, and Spiros raised his fist again. As he knocked the second time, the door swung open and a tall, thin man in black stood there, a dazed look on his face as if he had been sleeping or maybe in deep contemplation.

'Spiro, my son – welcome.' The papas greeted him. 'And...?' he looked at Vasso.

194

'Papas, this is Vasso. She is to be my bride. But she doubts me and so I want to prove the sincerity of my words by arranging our marriage.'

'Well, good evening to you, Vasso.' He did not seem put out or surprised by Spiro's speech but he did pause and look from the one to the other. 'I wondered who would manage to capture our Spiros. Come in, I want to meet you.' And he opened the door wider so they could enter the dark passageway. Inside, it smelt of musty books, and incense. The only light there was gleamed from under a door that presumably led to the room whose shutters emitted the glow they had seen from outside. Spiros moved towards it first, as if he had been there before.

The room was lit by two candles. There were four padded chairs with wooden arms and legs and two tables. The tables were stacked with books, and books lined the walls on purpose-built shelves. Over a crude plaster fireplace hung a regulation picture of Christ but the room was very obviously a shrine to knowledge.

'So, Vasso, you've taken Spiro's heart, have you?' The priest asked.

She did not answer.

'No need to be shy. Spiros and I are old friends. When he was a boy, still at school, he came here a lot, did you not, Spiro? Such a keen mind.' He picked up a book to give emphasis to his words, and put it down again. As he replaced it, a puff of dust rose and fell in the candlelight.

'She does not believe me, Papa,' Spiros said.

'And I do not believe that,' the priest answered. 'Women have fine instincts. She knows. Don't you, my dear?' He turned back to Vasso.

For a moment she felt caught. She knew, of course she knew. She had known from the moment she first laid eyes on Spiros that this was her man for life. So what was her doubt? She wondered if he would remain focused. Her fear was that she and the baby would be forgotten for his cooking.

'So, if you know, why the hesitation?' he asked her, having seemingly read the emotions on her face.

'Papas, I believe him. I believe what he says, but I also think he is drawn to prove himself. For this I think all his time and energy will be taken by his work.'

196

'Well, that is true. He is not a lazy man. But would you want a lazy man?'

'With respect, Papas, that is an unfair question that dismissed what I said.' As soon as the words were out she felt shocked at her boldness.

'Oh, she is a sharp one, Spiro. You will have to watch this one. I think you have chosen well!' He turned back to Vasso. 'I think that Spiros is a man who becomes driven by things and all his focus, all his energy, is thrown into whatever that interest is. That is the way I have always known him to be, and, to be good at a thing, that is how it has to be. As a consequence, Spiros has always been good at whatever he has turned his hand to. Before he started cooking he raised canaries. Did he tell you about that?'

Vasso shook her head.

'Well, that is a tale for him to tell you. Maybe when winter comes and you two are curled up beside the fire he will tell you all about it. But he became the best on the island, aged about twelve, I think, at breeding canaries, because he put his whole mind and soul into it. That is who he is.'

There was a pause as the papas looked at Spiros as if seeing the child he once was.

'So, if you have captured this man's heart and he has said that it is so, then, Vasso, my child, you can believe him and you can believe that you have all of his heart and he will be dedicated to you, body and soul. You see, I believe that all the energy he threw into canaries and cooking with his mama was all about finding a place to lay his heart with safety. A place of rest, a safe haven. It is natural that, now, as a mature man, this habit of his, this love of doing things well, will bubble to the surface through his work. But when he has a ring upon your finger, I have no doubt at all that what he will want to do well at will be providing for you and any children you may have.'

Vasso felt a heat in her cheeks and she hoped it did not show. Spiros glanced at her.

'Am I speaking out of turn, Spiro?' The papas asked, oblivious in the dim candlelight to Vasso's discomfort. 'Am I right?'

'You are exactly right, Papa,' Spiros said. 'So let's get that ring on her finger.'

'Well, I can see no reason to rush, Spiro.' the papas said.

'Ok, we will give it a week, then.'

'Ah, these things cannot be hurried. I will need a letter, a reference for Vasso – from the priest of her village, for example.

'Papas, we are not ruled by the Turks now. We are not back in those days. We are a modern country now. The post is quick. A day, two at the most!'

'Well, yes, but we will need a civil marriage licence.'

'Are you making obstacles, Papa?' Spiros chuckled.

'It is just that I have such a lot to do.' The papas said this rather wistfully, looking around at the table of books.

'Papa, you have always had such a lot to do! That table of books only gets added to. You will never feel you have read enough or know enough, so set them aside. They will wait for another day, but let me be married!'

The papas smiled, took his hand off the book it rested on, and did something between a wriggle and a shuffle in his chair, during which time his eyebrows lifted and he looked several years younger.

'I will, then,' he said, as if it was him being asked to get married.

'So – when?' Spiros stuck to his question, and Vasso, by this time, had a smile that creased the corners of her eyes. She was not sure if the feeling in her stomach was excitement or the baby letting its presence be known.

Chapter 25

A letter came from her mama to say that she, and about half the village, wanted to come for the celebration and was there anywhere they could stay? Stamatis listed over a dozen friends who would welcome Vasso's family and friends as their personal guests. This was not only the merging of two people, he said – it was a joining of two villages.

Argyro made the guest room over to Vasso: a light, bright room with a view of the sea. But, as it sat over some outbuildings beside the main house, it was very definitely separate, and she missed Spiro's evening visits and their loving nights in her little room in the courtyard at the back of the taverna. All eyes were upon them now, and everywhere she went, as she explored the town, people she did not know nonetheless knew her, and it also seemed that everybody was doing something for the wedding. It gave her a sense of belonging and a feeling of importance, but also a distant feeling as though she was in a dream. Lace was being made for the dress by nimble-fingered women who kept lace shops near the port. Flowers were being organised for the church by some cousins of cousins of Spiro's. The church itself, the one up by the windmill, would not hold more than twenty people, but no one seemed concerned. All of the harbour front was to be given over to the wedding feast and, as other tavernas were becoming involved, Spiro's plans for the celebration grew. Chairs and tables were stacked in readiness, the use of ovens in nearby tavernas was promised, food was shipped in, and Spiros was in complete command of everything, just as she had anticipated.

Vasso eagerly awaited her mama so she could feel a part of something, no longer a spectator, but when her mother disembarked from the fishing boat, along with a number of cousins and many more villagers than Vasso had anticipated, she almost didn't recognise them. It was not that her mama had aged or changed, but rather that she herself had changed. Her outlook had altered. Now her mama looked – well, as if she came from a poor farming village, which of course she did. But for some reason the rough weave of her faded black skirt, the hand-stitching of her greying blouse, came as a shock to Vasso. They were details she had not remembered.

'Mama!' she called, and as soon as she was in her mother's embrace it all came back to her and she was a stranger no longer.

'I am so proud of you, my love,' her mama had whispered in her ear.

'I hope you like him,' Vasso had muttered in return within the same embrace.

'If he makes you happy he is the best man in the world and I already love him,' her mama had replied, and their hug tightened, and they only separated when a suitcase being pulled from the boat nearly knocked them both off balance.

Spiros and Stamatis charmed the old woman; even Argyro greeted her pleasantly, but with a small knowing smile. A smile that repeatedly crept onto her lips, keeping Vasso in a state of unrest.

Naturally, Stella came, and with her there was none of the reluctance that Vasso experienced with her mama. Stella's presence was a relief, and Vasso found she could fully let her guard down as soon as they found a moment alone, and talk as if they had never been apart. Vasso caught up with the village gossip, and Stella asked never-ending questions about the ways of the islanders, Spiro's character and the chronology of his and Vasso's courtship, as well as teasing her about her impending wedding night. But she did not tell Stella about the baby. Somehow she felt that, for now, it was something only she and Spiros should know about.

Finally, the day came. Everything was ready. Vasso did not believe it was happening and the look of pride on her mama's face was a sight she would not have missed for the world.

As she wriggled into her wedding dress, she was aware of the slight curve to her belly.

'Would you look at that!' her mama said. 'For years I've been trying to fatten you up but after just a short time with the man you love you are more rounded and almost have a belly.' Then she laced the dress up and fussed over the veil.

The lace was thicker and heavier than Vasso had been expecting. It was a traditional lace of cotton thread, looped and twisted around nimble fingers. The end result was intricate but not fine and, as the cotton was not spun to a smooth texture, the resulting lace had a degree of coarseness. But the effect of the veil was beautiful, natural, and, as far as Vasso was concerned, transforming.

'Oh, you look so beautiful,' Mama had exclaimed, and then she had cried, which set off Stella and then Vasso's cousins, until all the women in the room except Vasso were weeping and wailing.

Stamati's donkey carried her sedately to the church, with people lining the way and filling every corner of flat space outside. As she had no one to give her away she had asked Stamatis if he would lead her to the church. He stood in his Sunday best, fidgeting awkwardly but looking handsome.

'That is how Spiros will look when we are older,' she whispered to herself, and she felt such happiness she thought she wouldn't be able to contain it all.

Sliding from the donkey, with Stamati's hands around her waist, she thought she caught a sneering look from Argyro, but the curl of the woman's lips quickly turned into a smile and Vasso decided she might have been mistaken. Still, she ignored her – the only person Vasso wanted to see was Spiros.

He was inside, smiling, as she entered, and his smile made her stomach turn over and her pulse race. The world around receded till there was no one but him in existence, and from the way he looked at her it seemed he could see only her. She became lost in his gaze and the whole process of the wedding, the prayers of the papas, the vows they took, the exchanging of crowns – even the three times around the altar, with all that rice being thrown at them – seemed to pass as if it wasn't really happening.

The olive-leaf crowns that Dimitri had circled and swapped over Vasso's and Spiro's heads had been intricately woven by the old ladies who made the lace, and everyone agreed the natural look of them enhanced the couple's good looks. A great amount of rice was thrown and some of the children had to be cautioned about not throwing it too hard. After the ceremony the happy couple and the best man made a small tour of the tiny church and back out under the blue skies. A couple of times Vasso almost wondered if it was a dream, especially when she caught her mama's huge smile as she dabbed her eyes. But Spiros had hold of Vasso's hand and he was not letting go. The rings were there, the deed had been done, and he kissed her as if she might escape if he did not make a lasting impression on her lips. But he had no need to worry. She was one with him, and no one beyond the two of them mattered. She had vowed to be with him all his life and he with her, and whatever doubts she had had up till now were as nothing.

They walked back to the harbour with the whole town following. Still more handfuls of rice were thrown and her lace veil became even heavier as the hard grains stuck in the holes. But she did not care; although, as they drew near to the port, a part of her anticipated the resentment she would feel at being alone for the next few hours as Spiros fussed over the preparation and serving of the food, in that moment she could not imagine being happier, or anyone or anything shattering their happiness.

So when they turned the corner and all the harbour front was laid out with tables with clean white cloths, a spray of orange bougainvillea in a wine carafe on each, the beauty of it all was so unexpected it brought tears to Vasso's eyes. Now Spiros would squeeze her hand and rush inside to manage the food. There would be *kokkinisto* – slow-roasted beef in a rich tomato sauce – with mountains of rice and salads made with fresh tomatoes and cucumber, and, of course, endless amounts of local wine. When the squeeze came, she was ready to let go – but Spiros didn't. Instead, he leaned towards Stamatis and exchanged a few quiet words, and it was her new father-in-law and the other taverna owners who hurried inside to see to the food and Spiros who led her to the head table under the clock tower.

'So beautiful,' he whispered, and kissed her jaw line – a little embarrassed, it seemed, for his loving action to be the focus of so many.

She could not have been more in love at that moment, and she took his hand under the table and put it on her belly.

Chapter 26

Down at the port they ate, drank ouzo and local wine, and danced, and it seemed that everyone on the island joined them. Although only a handful of people had actually been able to fit inside the tiny church, everyone agreed that the ceremony had been one of the most beautiful they had ever witnessed.

Speeches were given and largely ignored, and the wine flowed. Stamatis became very drunk, and the drunker he got the more he grinned, until finally he was taken home, arms over the shoulders of two friends, still smiling but with his eyes closed.

Vasso was kissed on the cheeks a thousand times over, and had blessings whispered in her ear, and Spiros never left her side. When the celebration was at its height he danced her down to the water's edge, and when no one was looking they slipped away back home, eager to consolidate their vows.

The morning saw them take the early boat across to the mainland, where they changed ferries and headed for the rocky outcrop of Monemvasia, where they would spend their honeymoon.

As they approached the peninsula from the north and landed at the mainland town, they saw nothing of the deserted village of Monemvasia itself, nestled on the sheltered southern slopes of the domed outcrop.

They arrived tired and hungry and agreed to find a place to stay and then get something to eat before exploring. Houses advertising rooms to let lined the waterfront. The first place they enquired at was full, but the kindly woman pointed around the bay, past two fish tavernas, to where her sister had rooms to rent. Vasso was glad that she had changed into sensible shoes and grateful that Spiros was carrying the bags. The room they found was spotlessly clean but both Vasso and Spiros agreed, with giggles, that the decoration was more suited to their yiayias than to people of their age. Handmade lace dollies adorned all the wooden surfaces. Along a shelf, folded and cut sheets of newspaper provided a replaceable, decorative covering, and there were several plastic vases in the shape of swans that displayed faded handmade paper tissue flowers.

After exploring the room their laughter subsided and Spiros declared, 'I think I might have overdone things yesterday.' His hands were in the small of his back and he flexed his shoulders.

'And you never stopped with the preparations!' Vasso added, massaging his neck.

'Do you mind if we rest a while before we go out to eat?' he asked, and he lay down, smoothing the sheets next to him for her to join him, and then closed his eyes. She must have been tired too, because when she woke the blue of the sky through the window had turned to navy. Spiros was grimacing and rubbing his chest.

'Are you alright?' Vasso asked.

'Sure.' He stopped rubbing. 'Hungry, I guess.'

The taverna had tables right by the water's edge, and, as they ate, hopeful fish gathered and fought for scraps of bread. The shoal heaved and writhed, fighting for the food, some fish sliding up the backs of others and out of the water to secure the morsels. The larger pieces were nudged and chased to the rocks where tiny crabs waited to seize the opportunity to pull the soggy dough into crevices, or higher onto the rocks where the fish could not reach.

A cat wound round their chairs and Spiros delighted in feeding the silent guest.

At one point, limping across the road to the tables, came a dog, its back leg dragging and useless.

'Oh, the poor thing,' Spiros said and gave it a succulent morsel. It ate eagerly and waited for more but, when no more came, their plates empty, it bounded away, no sign of a limp.

'Did you see that?' Vasso said, as the waiter brought a plate of watermelon.

'Ah, him. He's smart dog, don't believe his games. One day a leg, the next a paw – he is as crafty as a gypsy!' The waiter hissed and stamped his foot at the dog who was now trying the same tactic on other diners.

Spiros took Vasso's hand.

'When our little one is born we shall bring him–'

'Or her,' Vasso interjected.

'Or her – here to see the naughty clever dog?' His thumb rubbed across her knuckles and they both knew it was time to return to the hotel.

After sleeping deliciously late they rose together and made their way to see Monemvasia itself.

'I've heard that it's nothing but ruined buildings, built a very long time ago. I'm not sure what there is to see, but they say it is very beautiful. I think it was built there because they could easily protect themselves. At the top of the rock is a fort, but the main town is on a rocky slab by the sea,' Spiros told her.

Vasso didn't really care. She had her prizes with her, one holding her hand and another in her belly.

They walked across the causeway that joined the island to the mainland. The road around its perimeter went only one way and they followed it anticlockwise, vertical rock on their left and the sea on their right. They kept walking until they reached a decorated arch in the city walls, which led through to the narrowest cobbled path, with a sweet little bakery on the left and a shop selling handmade souvenirs on the right.

'So much for it being ruins,' Vasso quietly commented, as a woman in black, standing in the next doorway, asked them if they wanted to rent a room for the night. The doorway was tiny and they would have to bend to avoid bumping their heads, if they were to enter.
'Breakfast included,' she added, as they thanked her and moved on. On either side of the narrow street the cottages butted up against each other,

with occasional gaps where steps led up to the next street or down to the sea.

Although the houses on this main street were in good order, many of those away from the centre were in ruins, with crumbling stone walls and roof beams exposed to the sky. In many places the narrow lanes were blocked with bags of sand or cement. Signs on the main street advertised hotels and gift shops.

'I bet it was wonderful before the tourists took over.' Vasso ran her hand along the cornerstones of a building. 'Look how they do the doorways, so low and then with the quarter-circle pieces facing in at the top corners. Normally, the curve would go the other way to round the opening.' She laughed. 'I bet I would endlessly bump my head on those!'

At the far end, the narrow street opened into an area of rough, boulder-strewn ground with a high castle wall around it.

'You know what Monemvasia means, right?' Spiros asked.

'I've never thought – but *mone* means one or only... and *emvasia* as in to transfer or enter. I don't get it. Oh, yes I do! One entrance.'

They looked up at the wall that signified the end of their walk in that direction. Two men were perched precariously on top, restoring the fortifications and talking loudly. At one point in the wall was a heavy wooden door, tightly fastened.

'Well, when they have finished that, they will have to call it Diploemvasia,' said Spiros, and as Vasso worked out his joke he grabbed her hand and turned back the way they had come.

'There's not really much here, is there?' she commented.

'Let's go up this path,' said Spiros, and he led the way up a set of worn stone steps, which ended in a small courtyard where a woman in her nightdress was sharpening a pair of scissors on a stone.

'*Kalimera*,' Spiros greeted her.

The woman glanced briefly at her nightgown, but quickly looked up with a broad grin.

'*Kalimera*. You are taking a walk?' She smiled again and then resumed sharpening her scissors. 'You know, they come down from Athens but they do not care.' Spiros and Vasso looked at each other, unclear of her meaning, but happy enough to be there, in each other's company, sharing this experience. 'It is not their sweat that has restored our ancestors' home,' she continued, 'so why should they, I suppose.' She smiled as she spoke, as if the culprits were already forgiven. 'My children are not so bad.

They leave their towels and clothes about the place, as if there is a maid to pick up after them. But the grandchildren! Look what they did to my scissors.' And she happily ground the blunt edge against a stone. '"We are cutting wood to make a bridge," they told me. I had not realized what they were doing. You should see my chair!'

'Are you from here, then?' Vasso asked.

'I was born here, and raised here, but I got married and lived in Athens for… Oh, many years!' She waved her hand in a circular motion, as if the years were too many to count. Vasso noticed that a tiny sprig of rosemary was caught in the woman's hair and she wondered if she should offer to remove it.

'Then he died and now I am alone. They come to visit me but Athens is a long way.'

'You have neighbours?' Vasso asked, with a twinge of concern that the woman might be lonely.

'Neighbours! Ha!' She waved a dismissive arm at the only house within view that was not a ruin. 'The people who have bought that are French, and never here.' Then she pointed at a crumble of walls. 'There,' she said, 'are Germans, but they do not repair. And here are Americans, who come every two years or so for a week.'

'Are you lonely?' Vasso could not hold her question back. Spiros squeezed her hand, perhaps wanting to move on.

'Oh, no!' The woman was emphatic. Spiros released his tight grasp and looked up at the wall of rock that towered over the town. 'I was loved, you see, by such a good man.'

Spiros gave another little tug, more clearly a suggestion that they should move on, but Vasso held her ground.

'I think when you have been loved, truly and deeply, there is no room for loneliness. You can remember and recall. I still talk to him as if he is here, and I know what he would reply, his humour.' She laughed. 'I think it is when they have never experienced a meeting of minds that people get lonely. They do not miss so much what they had, but what they never had, do you know what I mean?' She looked long and hard at Vasso. 'Then, when their partner is gone they can afford to mourn for the connection they never had in the guise of mourning for the partner.' She rolled her eyes as if such behaviour was futile. 'But sometimes when I would just like a cuddle I have to wait for my children to visit.'

'What's that?' Spiros changed the subject, pointing at a cave high up in the rock face.

'Ah!' The woman put down her scissors. 'A very holy place! Years ago an icon was found there. No one had put it there, it was a miracle!'

'Is it still there?' Vasso asked.

'It is a dedicated church now, and there are many icons.'

'Come, Vasso, let's have a look.' Spiros seized the chance to leave.

'Yes, take a little walk,' the woman encouraged, 'but be careful. The way is steep and at the top very narrow. Light a candle for me.'

'Come with us, show us the way,' Vasso gently teased the woman whose back was too bent to go far and whose slippers would not have managed the rough track up the hillside.

'Ach! I am too old now. You young people go.' And she returned to sharpening her scissors, with a smile on her lips.

As Vasso began to climb, she could hear the woman talking to herself. 'They asked me to show them the way! Can you imagine, with my knees, but do you remember the times we went up there before the children were born?'

Her voice faded as Spiros led the way around the corner of the final house on the slope. Before them now were boulders and loose stones, tufts of dried grass.

'I think if we go up that way it will lead to the track you can see further up.' Spiros said, and before his words were finished he was off, putting distance between them.

The going was hard. Some parts were very steep and the stones beneath her feet tended to slide. There was nothing to hold on to. Spiros was a good distance ahead and so she continued, pausing to catch her breath as the way became even steeper, until finally she was climbing using sharp handholds and loose crevices for her feet.

'Be careful,' she called up to Spiros, but the breeze and the rocks swallowed her words. She emerged onto a narrow track that hugged the cliff. Spiros was leaning against the rock face, his hand on his chest, and his face was contorted.

'Spiro? Are you alright?' Vasso panted.

'Yes, just wanted to look at the view for a moment.' His hand still held his chest.

'Do you have a pain?'

'No, no, nothing like that. Just a bit of indigestion. Look, the path becomes very narrow against that rock face.'

'Ah, but there is a wall.'

'It's ankle-high. It will stop your feet slipping. Are you sure you want to go on?'

'Don't you? Is the pain bad?'

219

'There is no pain now.' He let go of his chest, but a darkness crossed his eyes; there *was* something. 'You go ahead and I will follow, unless you are scared.' There was a teasing note to his voice.

The way forward looked exciting and she could not wait.

'Go, I will follow in a second.' He dismissed her and his gaze roamed over the huge expanse of sea below them.

The way was narrow and Vasso kept her back to the wall of rock. The cave entrance was small and inside was whitewashed and decorated with icons in frames hung from rusting nails. There were also *tamata* – palm-sized square tin plates that had been hammered out into primitive pictures. One showed a knee, another a baby, and another a crutch. These, too, hung from nails on what once would have been colourful ribbons, now faded with time. An altar had been laid out on a slab of rock, with a bottle of oil, the base of an oil lamp, a box of matches.

Spiros crossed himself three times as he came in. He looked at everything in silence and then took Vasso's hands to look in her eyes.

The way he looked at her suggested he saw more deity there than in any of the relics, and Vasso felt a little irreligious. His look told her that he would be part of her forever and he would never stop loving her or idolising her, no matter what the future brought. It was such an intense and fierce look that Vasso felt slightly afraid, and in her fear she released one of her hands from his and placed it protectively over her belly. Her movement broke the spell and he smiled and felt her belly too, laughing now. Back out in the sunshine they slipped and slid their way back to the town and hurried back to the rented room.

Chapter 27

The honeymoon felt like it was over before it began, but, once back on Orino Island, Vasso found that the room above the outbuilding, now their room, was all the nicer for Spiros being there. They were together by day in the taverna and also together at night. In the few days after their return, Stamatis was ever cheerful and Argyro was mostly silent. Whilst they were away, Stamatis said, the taverna had been quiet but with Spiros back it was becoming busier by the day. It seemed everyone wanted a repeat of the tastes they had enjoyed during the festivities.

'Argyro, have you ordered more beans? We have very few tomatoes left, and the onions we have are soft.' Argyro thumbed through her latest magazine.

'I've ordered them from Panayiotis.'

'Panayiotis! Why, Argyro? His quality is not good. Please could you-'

'Don't start, Spiro. I have ordered what I think is right. You go off on your honeymoon and do not give us a thought and then you come back and parade behind your counter thinking the whole show is about you. This is a business we are running.'

'And we are busy, and to continue to be busy we need to have quality ingredients.'

'The books have to balance. Where do you think the money came from to feed so many at your wedding?'

'Out of my pocket!' Spiros snapped back.

'You mean from the earnings you took when you used this place as your own, paying no rent? You call that your money, do you?' Argyro snarled.

'I bought the ingredients, good ingredients too. None of the wilted, flavourless stuff Panayiotis has.'

'Which is fine when you are cooking for a wedding or for one or two friends, but this is a business we are running. Besides, there isn't only us now, there is also her.' She pointed her cigarette at Vasso. 'And soon there will be another mouth to feed as well.'

'If we do not have good ingredients we will lose all our trade. Tell Panayiotis we do not want that order.'

223

'Please stop!' Vasso found her voice.

They did. They stopped and stared at her.

Vasso had noted a shift in Spiros since their honeymoon, since that day on Monemvasia, in the cave up on the hillside. She had tried to persuade herself that it was in her imagination but the more time passed the clearer it was that something had changed. Hearing him now, standing up to Argyro, cemented these thoughts, but for now he would have to work it out for himself. Her concern was the unborn child.

'They say even babies in the womb can hear everything. Please don't let him hear this.'

'It was only a matter of time, wasn't it?' Argyro snapped.

'What was?' Spiros asked.

'Before she started to feel superior because she is pregnant, and now she is telling us what to do, using the baby as a weapon. I saw this coming.'

'That is unfair, Argyro. Vasso neither feels superior not wants to tell us what to do. That is not who she is at all. How could you say such a thing?'

'All women are like that. Get them pregnant and they start to act like they are something special, like they have done something clever.'

'This is not about Vasso at all, is it? This is about you, Argyro!' Spiros faced her, fists clenched.

'What sort of man are you, Spiro! To throw it in my face that I cannot have children? What sort of monster would do that? It makes me terrified to think what sort of baba you are going to make.'

'Oh!' Vasso cried out.

'What is it?' Spiros dropped his tongs on the grill and hastened around to her side. She stood looking at the floor. At her feet, a chip of marble, displaced from the smooth floor, proved the force of the falling knife and the sharpness of its point.

'I'm alright. I just dropped it,' Vasso said, Spiro's arm around her.

'And yesterday you dropped a bowl on your foot.' Spiros spoke kindly, with a small laugh, designed to put her at ease.

'And a whole plate of food,' Argyro chipped in, with no laugh, just a hard stare.

'I do feel a little clumsy these days,' Vasso whispered to Spiros, quietly enough that Argyro could not hear.

'I will not have you whispering about me when I am in the room.' Argyro stood sharply, knocking her coffee so that it slopped over the rim and her cigarette rolled from the saucer she was using as an ashtray onto the floor.

'Stop it, Argyro, it was not about you,' Spiros implored.

'Then why whisper?'

'I cannot do this, Spiro,' Vasso whispered again. 'Not with the baby inside me, I feel stressed and, oh…' She bent double.

'Vasso! Are you are alright?"

'What is it, son?' Stamatis came in from outside.

'Vasso indulging in some dramatics,' Argyro replied.

'Does it hurt?' Spiros asked. 'Is it the baby?'

'Panayia!' Stamatis called on his god and was by Vasso's side. Father and son took an arm each and they led her to the chair where Argyro was sitting, just staring at them.

'Get up, woman,' Stamatis spat, and the startled Argyro stood and moved aside as they sat Vasso down. Spiros squatted on the floor in front of her.

'Do you need a doctor?' he asked.

'No,' Vasso said cautiously, and then a smile came to her lips. 'No, but you need to feel.' She put his hand on her stomach and smiled up at Stamatis. 'I think it just kicked.' Stamatis waited his turn to feel and the three of them tried to make out the baby's foot, and then maybe where the head might be. They tried to guess if it was a girl or boy and, after a few minutes, Vasso became very aware of Argyro standing staring at the three of them.

'You want to feel?' she said.

Argyro's finger's twitched but then she frowned and made no move to come closer.

'You know, it might be time for you to stop work, Vasso. If anything happened I would never forgive myself,' Spiros said.

'It's early days yet.' She tried to get to her feet.

'No, Vasso, Spiros is right. Argyro can do the washing-up,' Stamatis agreed.

'But what will I do all day?'

Spiros leaned towards her and whispered. 'We will find you a magazine to read,' and he tried very hard not to laugh.

Argyro could not have heard, but she banged some pots around to show her displeasure anyway.

Chapter 28

The next day Stamatis was at the taverna before anyone else, and he had made some changes. The table by the counter, Argyro's table, now had a tablecloth on it and, where the ashtray had been the day before, he had placed a glass with a bright pink sprig of bougainvillea in it. A magazine, more colourful than any Argyro tended to read, with a young French face adorning the front cover, lay unopened.

'I bought her this.' Stamatis left the pile of knives and forks he was wrapping in napkins ready to lay on the tables and unfolded something on the chair next to him. It was a full-length apron with pink flowers and blue edging. 'So her clothes don't get wet when she washes up.'

'It might take more than that to soften Argyro, Baba,' Spiros said.

'It's lovely.' Vasso offered her support of her father-in-law's actions. But the look on

228

Stamati's face told her he was afraid it was not going to make the situation any easier.

'But you, Vasso,' Stamatis found his smile. 'This table is for you.' He pulled out the chair so she could sit. 'I didn't know what you like to read so I got one with a girl on the cover that looked like you.'

Vasso looked at this girl in her false eyelashes and her red lipstick and could not help but chuckle. But her hand went to her hair. Maybe she could wear a little make-up sometimes. A woman should not let herself go just because she was married.

'Ha! Thank goodness it isn't!' Spiros laughed and then stood behind Vasso as she opened the first page, all of them intrigued by the novelty and the bright colours of the glossy production. Spiros had seemed like his old self then, and the change that had occurred on the honeymoon faded a little and Vasso felt they were back at a place where they had no secrets from each other.

They were still standing this way when Argyro came in, and her face could not have made her feelings any more obvious. Stamatis presented the apron along with many soothing words, and she took it in silence and began a slow clattering that lasted all day.

The pattern was repeated the next day, and the day after that, and Argyro became more and more silent. Spiros seemed to forget that she was even there as he talked to Vasso. He spoke of the baby, of what they would do with the rooms below their bedroom when they had enough money to buy materials. There was a sense of urgency in his words even though his tone was steady, and it reminded Vasso of something that she could not quite put her finger on. He wanted to build a kitchen, of course, but also a room where the baby could crawl and play, he insisted. Vasso felt she should be pleased with these plans, but somehow she was unsettled instead.

Time passed and mostly the days were peaceful. Then one day Vasso felt a sharp cramp before she was even out of bed.

'What's the matter?' Spiros asked as she sat up and twisted to put her feet on the floor

'Just a little cramping, but it's really painful.'

Spiros left immediately and returned with the pharmacist, who called his friend the doctor and the doctor ordered her back to bed.

'For how long?' Vasso asked, and he shrugged.

And so she stayed at home. Stamatis brought her a magazine and coffee every morning. Spiros popped back once or twice to chat and stroke her face, but the days were long and lonely.

Chapter 29

The real pain came just after they had gone to bed one evening. The first was just a weak pulse, but the second had her gripping the sheets.

'I can't do this!' she had called out.

Spiros, always quick to fall asleep, was already gently snoring, and he awoke with a start.

'Is it time?' He pushed back the thin sheet that had been keeping off the mosquitoes.

The pain had stopped.

'Oh, that was a bit extreme, but I think that was a one-off. No, it has passed. Sorry to wake you.'

She looked into his eyes, which were wide and scared.

'Don't worry, Spiro. Women have been doing this for thousands of years. It is… Oh my, no, I can't do this. No!'

'Hold me,' Spiros demanded, and she felt for him and her arms went around his shoulders and she rode the pain coursing down the other side, so close to Spiros.

Then they waited for the next spasm, but nothing happened. They waited some more and still nothing.

'You know, I've been thinking, for when the baby comes. I mean, I've been busy, but it's just nicer when you're in the taverna as well,' Spiros said. It sounded like he had a point to make, something he was working up to saying, but Vasso could not concentrate on his words; her whole being was focused on what her body needed.

'Do you think we should let the midwife know? I understand it's the donkey man's mama? If she is at their home up on the ridge it might take her an hour to get here.'

'She'll only come if it's a difficult birth. Baba's cousin said she would come if you wanted help. Shall I get her?'

'Perhaps not yet.'

'So, I was thinking that it might be good for Argyro to give some of her time to the little one.

'Here it comes again. Hold me.' The spasm rode across her back, crescendoed until she thought she could bear no more and then retreated like a wave. 'I thought they were meant to come across your stomach?' she said, panting for breath.

'If she were to take him, or her, we could run the taverna together.'

'Spiro, I am not sure this is the time to talk of such things. Let's bring her, or him, into the world first.'

'It's just that she has offered…'

'What has she offered?' A flare of distrust rose in her, followed by another contraction. With her face in Spiro's shoulder she hung on and, rather like at her wedding, the world disappeared and there was only him, his shoulder, only his voice and the squeezing, the muscles in her body taking over and the huge desire to get the baby out, just get it out, to use every force within her to get it out.

'She says I can have the taverna if she can play her part in bringing him up.'

'Hold me, hold me, I need to get…' She shuffled to the edge of the bed.

'The taverna would be ours. Officially.'

'Oh, it's going, it's subsiding. Stay close. Don't let me go.'

'So shall we agree to that?'

'To what?'

'To Argyro giving us the taverna officially?'

'Really, did she say that?'

'Yes. She would hand over the books, get it changed at the tax office – everything.'

'Why?'

'Did you not hear me?'

'Hear what? Oh, hang on, here is, oh…'

'Breathe, breathe,' Spiros spoke into her ear and she felt like she was taking on the biggest job of her life. Closing her eyes, she focused on the baby's needs, focusing from the ends of her fingers and up from her toes, concentrating all her energy. Another spasm blocked out the world and there was only the desperate need to help the baby out. As the waves came closer together, she felt not so much a sensation of pain, but, rather, a determination to do the right thing for the baby – and also, with a pure animal urge, to get what was now a separate being out of her body. This added selfishness only built on the urges that were there already, her strength growing. To stop the experience totally engulfing her, she kept her face pressed into Spiro's shoulder and there was only him and his voice in the whole word. She could hear nothing else: just his voice, his breathing, his heartbeat.

'You're doing great, Vasso. Keep going my love.' His words soothed and washed over her.

'Perhaps get the cousin to come, to tie the cord. No, don't go, not now. Stay.' And she gripped him with the same strength that the waves gripped her and together they rode high above anywhere she had ever been before and there was only him. 'I love you!' She could hear her own voice echoing in the room and Spiros was laughing and shouting. 'It's a boy, he's a boy. Vasso, we have a son.' And they laughed and Spiros shouted out of the window for Stamatis who whooped his delight into the night. With the baby held against her she felt another wave.

'Why another wave, Spiro, what is happening?' And Spiro's eyes widened as Vasso grimaced. He took the baby as she strained and then the pain was gone.

'Am I too late?' The briefest of taps preceded the appearance of Stamati's cousin's head around the door. Spiros pulled a sheet over Vasso and an old woman came in, slightly stooped and holding a headscarf around a pleasant, age-worn face.

'Now, where have we got to? Oh my, she is here!'

'He!' Vasso and Spiros said in unison.

'Can I come in?' Stamatis called from outside the door.

'In a minute,' his cousin said, and the old woman deftly did all that was necessary, wrapping the child and dealing with the mess as best she could.

'I could do with a bucket of water, Stamatis.'

'Boiling water?' He asked through the door.

'No! I just want to clean the place up a bit. Perhaps you could manage some clean sheets, too.'

Vasso paid the cousin no attention. She had her son and her husband; her world was complete.

'You can come in now, Stamatis,' the old woman said and, to Vasso's shock, right behind Stamatis was Argyro. Vasso held on to her child tightly.

Stamatis reached down for the little bundle and he took it with such care it made Vasso smile. After gazing tenderly at his first grandchild he stepped forward and, bending down, offered him back.

'May I?' Argyro asked, and without waiting for a reply she pushed in and took the child from Stamatis, gazing closely at him, cooing and clucking over the little boy, rocking him and stroking his face with one finger.

Chapter 30

Argyro, her face so close to the baby's, walked towards the door on swaying hips.

'My baby!' Vasso squealed.

'Argyro?' Stamatis said.

Spiros was on his feet.

'Oh, look at you all, so jumpy. You're acting if I was going to steal him.' Argyro laughed. But she never took her eyes from her charge as she turned around and swayed back to the bedside.

'Please,' Vasso said and stretched out her arms.

'Who is a handsome boy then? Who is my handsome boy? What a beautiful boy you are.'

'Argyro!' Vasso stretched her hands even further.

Argyro continued to address the little bundle. 'Oh dear, his mama is quite jealous. Who's my boy, eh? Shall I give you back to Mama? Shall I? Or do you want another cuddle?'

'Argyro.' Stamatis was by her side, his arm around her shoulder. 'Let the baby suckle.' Finally, Argyro surrendered the boy and Vasso pulled him back to her breast.

'We've seen him now. Let's go back to our beds and leave this family to find their feet,' said Stamati's cousin. She wished them farewell but assured them that they must not hesitate to call her if she could do anything further.

'She's right. Come, Argyro.' And, as the three of them left, the room fell silent.

'Look what we did!' Spiros lay close to Vasso, pulling the blanket edge away from his son's face.

'She nearly walked out with him.'

'Look, he's yawning. So cute. And look at the size of his hands.'

'Did you see her?' Vasso asked.

'Have you counted his toes? Ah, how perfect. Look how they curl.'

'Is he gripping your finger with his toes?'

'Just about. How clever is he?'

'Oh, look at his little chubby knees.'

And the night passed with them inspecting their son from head to toe and being amazed by everything about him. He started to cry, but Vasso rocked him against her chest, and he found the source of nourishment and sighed himself into oblivious ecstasy.

The baby fell asleep against Vasso and Vasso fell asleep against Spiros, the three of them curled up on the bed. So when dawn came and Spiros tried to wriggle out for work Vasso woke and their baby woke. Again, the small child started to cry but Vasso was there ready to feed him, a fresh towel around him.

'I need to go to work.' There was that urgency again as Spiros spoke. 'I will come back as soon as the doors are open and I have left Baba with some instructions about what to prepare for me later.' He kissed her forehead.

Vasso took his words, his kiss, his thoughts, his kindness, but she did not care if he was going for an hour or a day. Her world was at her breast and he was all she needed right now.

'Do you want to call him Stamatis after your baba?' she asked casually, immune to his hurry.

'No, I don't think so. How about Theodoris after my grandfather?' he replied absently.

'Very traditional, but is there not some issue with your grandfather and Argyro? Won't that be a problem?'

'Ah, good point. Maybe I can ask Baba now what that is all about. It's a good excuse isn't it? I have to go, my sweet.' And he bent low and kissed his child on his forehead and then kissed Vasso's shoulder, and kissed her lips and kissed her nose and kissed her hand and left.

'You want to be a Theodoris? It's a nice name.' The baby cooed its answer and Vasso was amazed. 'Theodoris?' She said again and again the baby gurgled. 'I think you like it.'

Minutes after Spiros had gone, Stamatis announced his presence with a gentle knock. 'Can I come in?'

'Sure.' Vasso pulled the sheet over her and lifted the baby onto the outside.

'And how is our brave mama?' Stamatis asked.

'Isn't he perfect?' Vasso said.

'He is indeed perfect. Ach. I can still remember the day Spiros came into the world. Anna, my wife, looked more beautiful than I had ever seen her. And Spiros came into this world with a shock of hair you wouldn't believe!' His eyes clouded and he looked like he might cry. 'Anna was quite a woman.' He said it so quietly Vasso was not sure if he meant to speak it out loud.

'We're thinking of calling him Theodoris, after your baba,' Vasso offered.

He reacted as if coming out of a dream.

'Theodoris?' But the clouded look was still partially there.

242

'Would that be alright? Because – well, I do not mean to go where I am not invited, but I have sort of understood that there is some kind of issue. I really don't want to make things worse – you know, with Argyro.'

'Ah yes,' Stamatis said, but without really listening. He was elsewhere and his fingers found the baby's hand, its tiny fingers trying to grip him.

'Stamatis?' She put her free hand on his shoulder and he lifted his head, his eyes swimming with tears. 'Oh.' She was not sure what to say, seeing the pain in his eyes.

'She was such a good woman. Kind, gentle, caring, soft, never raised her voice, and she could cook. Not this fancy stuff that Spiros does. Just plain, good food.'

'You must miss her.'

'Every day.' The baby made a gurgling sound.

'But now you have Argyro.' Vasso was trying to be kind but just saying it felt like a taunt. How could he have married someone like her after a wife who was so sweet and kind that just the thought of her reduced him to tears? Why would he marry someone like her?

'Argyro.' He almost sneered the word, and looked from the baby to the window, as if

243

he wanted to get away. 'What a bitter person she is.'

Vasso's mouth dropped open and her eyes widened. She quickly tried to wipe the shock from her face but he looked back and caught it.

'I know. You must wonder why I ever married her.'

'It's none of my business,' Vasso said, returning his gaze.

'It may not be, but I know you do.' His sadness filled the room, and she even forgot her beautiful son, just for a second.

'If she makes you this sad then why did you, Baba?' The word slipped out so naturally she found no reason to retract it or explain it.

'Normally, I would say this is no one's business but ours. Argyro's and mine.'

She waited.

'But seeing as you want to call the baby Theodoris I think you should know everything there is to know and then you can decide. I will not stop you.'

Part of Vasso did not want to know. If this gave Argyro excuses to behave as she did, it would not make life any easier to know it. It would just give her, Vasso, more to endure. But if it would help her to understand and sympathise with Stamatis, maybe she could listen. No one should be alone in their suffering.

'Tell me.' The words were uttered as an offering.

'I just hope you don't think less of me, Vasso. I value your regard, and I did what I did out of the best of motives. Maybe I was wrong, and maybe what I did was cruel but, if you lose your soul mate like I lost Anna, God forbid, you don't think straight. In my defence I will say that I saw no future life for me, even though Spiros was still only young. I saw no personal future for me, so to use my life to benefit another seemed the best thing to do. At least, that's what I thought I was doing. I think in reality I may have made everything worse.'

'I don't think I quite follow, Stamatis.'

'No, why would you? You see, my mama had just given birth to me and, naturally, my baba, Theodoris, was elated. Theodori's best friend Augustinos was celebrating the announcement of the pregnancy of his wife, with Argyro.'

Chapter 31

Two metal tables stood on the uneven flags in front of the boat shed, on the harbour front. The double doors, large enough for a fishing boat to pass through, stood open, and the light from the bare bulb inside shone on the stones outside, making them sparkle where the spray from the sea had reached. At the back of the boat shed, nets and other fishing paraphernalia were piled up, but towards the front there were more tables and wooden chairs with rush-work seats, and a makeshift counter where Augustinos served Greek coffee in tiny cups and shots of ouzo and brandy to the fishermen. A wood burner had been installed in one corner, and a large group of men were huddled around this at one of the tables, playing cards and laughing. All the other tables were occupied, too, with groups of two or three.

'Have you finished yet?' Theodoris sat heavily on one of the chairs outside. The night sky was spotted with stars but clouds kept blowing in front of the moon, darkening the harbour. Olive oil lamps on the two tables flickered their own yellow light and spat and hissed as the raw wicks burnt.

'New Year's Eve?' Augustinos laughed. 'What do you think! People will be drinking till dawn. There is a card game over there that has been going on since six this evening. Or rather, since yesterday. What time is it?'

'About three!' Theodoris answered, noting that every table had been equipped with a pack of cards to keep the New Year tradition alive. 'Come Augustinos, put down your tray and let's drink to my little Stamatis and your pregnant wife.'

'Ah yes!' Augustinos exclaimed, as if he had forgotten the baby that was soon to come to him.

'All those sitting here are friends, are they not? They will not object if you are a little leisurely in your work tonight.' Theodoris looked around the tables, at the people there who were his friends, his cousins, his neighbours, as they were Augustino's.

'I will buy you an ouzo from yourself.' Theodoris laughed. 'In fact, bring the bottle!' Whilst he waited he looked to the sky and thought about Stamatis, his little dark head, his wide-eyed stare, and wondered who he would be as a man.

'What are you pondering?' Augustinos returned and sat down, put the cloth he always held in his hand on the next chair and uncorked the ouzo.

'I was thinking about little Stamatis, wondering what his life will be like. If it will differ from mine,' Theodoris said.

'Of course it will differ from yours. Life is different for every generation, and, as you said yourself, it is only a matter of time before plastic chairs take over from the wooden ones. It is not likely he will follow you in your trade. You should bring some plastic chairs onto the island yourself, Theodoris, sell them, make yourself a new trade. They can be wiped clean, and there is no need to paint them year after year, and no need to repair them. I'm sorry to say, but soon your work is finished, my friend.'

'Ah well, there are always your chairs.' Theodoris felt along the edge of the rush seat he was sitting on. These rushes he had harvested and stripped and soaked until they were malleable, and had then woven over the wooden frame of the chair, building up the layers to make the seat comfortable and hard-wearing. Not everyone was permitted to collect the rushes, and all those years ago when he applied for his licence he thought it was a trade in which he could never lose out.

'Yes, well, I do need to talk to you about that, but not tonight. Tonight is New Year!'

'Talk about what, exactly?'

'Not now, Theodoris.'

'You are switching to plastic chairs?'

'It is only a thought. Most of mine need reworking and they all need repainting. It would just be easier, and cheaper, I'm afraid. There, I have said it. But it is not decided yet. Come, drink with me.'

Theodoris put his glass to his lips but he could not drink. His joy had turned to worry. No more repair work from Augustinos would be a serious blow. He didn't have a huge number of chairs but he had more chairs than anyone else on the island. It would be a big dent in his income if that stopped, and now he had a baby how would he manage?

'Drink, Theodoris. I didn't say I was swapping to plastic chairs... Just that – well, let us not talk of it now. *Yamas!*' And he chinked his glass against his friend's and they drank. Then they talked of their children, and of the year to come and what the new mayor might do, and of years past, but all the time Theodoris worried for his boy's future.

'*Yamas!*' The cry came from a dozen voices, from the group nearest the wood stove, who had been playing cards since six the previous evening. One of them beckoned Augustinos, who picked up his cloth and marched inside to bring more ouzo. He collected the empties and came back outside.

'Come, Theodoris,' he said to his friend. 'Let us celebrate the new year ourselves.' And he opened a pack of cards and shuffled them.

They played a few hands and they refilled their glasses. Worries were forgotten and the two friends talked of their schooldays, the mischief they got into and the teacher who came from the mainland, so young and pretty. They remembered the wicked things they did as teenagers, which they thought they had kept private from their parents only to find out years later that parents know most things about their children, especially on an island too small for secrets.

'I have run out of cigarettes.' Augustinos stood. 'I have some inside.'

'I have one here.' Theodoris slipped one out of his breast pocket, 'But I am not going to make this easy for you. You can play me for it.' And he dealt the cards. Augustinos won and they smoked together, looking out to sea. The wave tops caught the light of the moon when it appeared from behind the clouds. Jasmine, somewhere between the houses behind them, gave off its scent, elusive and subtle, and

Theodori's thoughts returned again to tiny Stamatis. He thought of the child's future, and then of his own.

'I'll tell you what.' Theodoris slurred his words. 'I will play for you not to take on plastic chairs this year.'

'And if I win?' Augustinos laughed before he spoke, a big belly laugh as if this was the funniest thing he had heard in ages. He, too, was drunk.

'I will repair half your chairs for free!'

'That is a rash promise, my friend.'

'I mean it. If you take plastic this year I will have none of your chairs to repair. This way I assure half my income.'

'But I never said I had decided.' Augustinos continued to chuckle.

'Then this is a way to decide.'

'Ok then!' He shuffled the deck and dealt. 'Why not!'

They began in good humour but, as the cards began to go against him, Theodoris realised what he had agreed to. If he lost, Augustinos would get plastic chairs, and if Augustinos did that others on the island would eventually follow suit. He could go out of business. It had been a bad judgement, thanks to too much ouzo. He slammed back another shot of the aniseed spirit and swallowed hard. Would Augustinos hold him to it? Irrelevant. He,

Theodoris, was a man of his word. If he lost he would keep his word even if Augustinos didn't want him to. It was a matter of principle.

'Let's up the stakes!' Theodoris roared.

'I think we've had too much to drink to up the stakes, my friend. Let us play on, but just for fun.' Augustinos chucked back his own ouzo and refilled the glasses. Close to his eye, the tic had started – the one Theodoris noticed he always got when he felt under pressure. Augustinos rubbed at it with his free hand but it did not go away.

'We cannot play on for fun. A bet has been made. I suggest we increase it! This could be a tremendous start to the new year.' Theodoris felt brave, seeing the tic.

'But only for one of us,' Augustinos replied, and they drank again, and again he refilled the glasses. 'Besides, I am not sure I could play another hand as I think there are two of you now.'

'It sounds to me like you are playing chicken.' Theodoris made a clucking sound, taunting Augustinos as each had done to the other back in school, and Augustinos laughed, but the glint in his eye told Theodoris that he had hit his mark.

'Alright then. So what shall we up this bet to?'

'If you win I fix all your chairs for free. And if I win you do not take plastic chairs for five years.'

'That's crazy! How do we know what will be happen in five years? They give out fewer fishing licences each year, and that means fewer fishermen in my cafe. Every year more people leave the island because there are no ways to make a living. The harbour front is exposed and cold during the winter and exposed and hot during the summer. I might not even have a cafe here in five years.'

'Ah, so you are scared, are you?'

'Certainly not, but that is a crazy bet. If I win you lose your entire income, but if you win I do not lose my entire income, so it is not even.'

'Okay then, so let's say that if you win then I will buy you the plastic chairs and the rest of the island will follow you and I will go out of business. But if I win I take your cafe and you take my business, and I do not buy plastic chairs.'

'You are talking like a madman,' Augustinos said with a laugh, and refilled both their glasses, the muscle by his eye twitching as he spoke.

'We can hear you!' A man at the next table called across. 'Is that Augustinos, playing chicken like he did back at school?'

Theodoris saw his friend bristle at this.

'What's the bet?' another from the same party called, and the whole table stopped their game to look over to Augustinos and Theodoris.

'I think the bet was a swap of jobs, wasn't it?'

'What, this boatshed Augustinos calls a cafe against a rush-cutting licence? What man would not jump at the chance, game or no game!'

'It's true.' Another spoke up. 'There's hardly a living to be made with a harbour side café. We fishermen are few and the coins we hold even fewer. Anyone with money sits in the better places, not out here, exposed to the elements. Take the bet and hope you lose, Augustinos.' And all the men at the table dissolved into laughter.

'Take the bet,' Theodoris pushed, but he was beginning to doubt himself and now he, too, was wondering whether he had offered a good business for a bad one. Yet just a minute ago it had seemed the other way around. However, the words had been spoken; he could not back out.

Chapter 32

'So your family won the taverna in a bet?' Vasso rocked the baby, even though he was asleep.

'It was not the same back in those days. There was no tourism, just fishermen on the front there. The bet really was the building for the rush-cutting licence. It was a closed profession and those licences were like gold, back in those days. But my baba, when he went to the mainland to cut the rushes, saw the future in the bigger towns. The plastic chairs were taking the place of the old wooden ones, and he was scared.'

'Still, it was a heavy bet.' Vasso shook her head in disapproval.

'Ach, there have been bigger bets, and crazier ones too. Last year an American lost his yacht to one of the Kaloyannis brothers in a game of cards at New Year.'

'Well, if Argyro's baba lost the building in a card game, does that really excuse her behaviour?' she said.

'Well, that is where I made my mistake. You see, the building had been earmarked for his unborn baby as a dowry, if it was a girl. So, the way Argyro sees it, her dowry was lost to my baba in a game of cards.'

'I can see how that might hurt.'

'Without a dowry she had less chance of marrying.'

'Yes.' Vasso nodded but something was still not clear. 'But really, once it was done, it was done.'

'Well, that is what I thought. The cafe was nothing when I was a youngster – a fisherman or two had a coffee there. Sure, it was full at New Year, or during a festival, but most of the time it was just a hobby. A way for him to pass the time. I mean, I grew up crawling on the floor of that café, but it was Anna's idea to turn it into a taverna. Tourism was at its height and the tourists wanted to sit where they could see the water. From a taverna there was a really good living to be made. I never even thought that making it a success would cause a problem.'

The baby murmured and Stamatis leaned over and kissed the small child's forehead.

'But you see, Anna was more sensitive than me. There was no interest from anyone to marry Argyro and after I married Anna she began to be spiteful. One day she so upset Anna, and Anna couldn't understand why Argyro would have anything against her. They didn't even know each other. So I told Anna everything. I wanted her to see that it wasn't her, you see? Do you know what she said?'

Vasso shrugged her shoulders gently.

'She said, "Stamatis, if we ever get the chance to make it right for her, we will." Can you imagine saying that after Argyro had been so mean? But that was Anna. A sweeter soul you could not imagine.' He stared blankly at the wall for a few moments.

'After Anna died, I forgot her words. From the moment of her death Argyro was here all the time, as if Anna had been a special friend of hers. I could not really understand her presence, but nor did I care. All I wanted was Anna, but that was impossible.' He paused and sighed as if he had no energy left for such a cruel world. Vasso wanted to say something sympathetic, but before she had thought of anything he spoke again. 'Life continued with me behind a black curtain. I could feel nothing of life and I felt dead. I had no future. Then, one day, and I forget what started it, but Argyro actually confronted me and accused my baba of stealing her dowry from her.' He said the words without malice but Vasso covered her mouth with her hand to hold in a gasp of surprise and horror. 'As her words struck me I remembered that it was Anna's wish that we should find a way to make it right and, just for a second, the first chink of light for weeks entered my world and I felt closer to Anna.' He physically relaxed as he said these words; his shoulders dropped, his neck extended a little; and then the tension returned as he continued. 'It closed as quickly as it had opened. I wanted to feel it again, but I knew Anna was gone, and I could still see no point in my life and the world was dark again.' Stamatis sighed, and paused for so long that Vasso began to wonder if he was going to say any more. After a while he looked up and resumed his monologue.

'Also, and this seemed very important at the time, Spiros had lost his mama. So, from a very sad place, thinking it would bring me closer to Anna and give Spiros a mama, I offered to marry Argyro. The brightness of being near Anna opened up again, just for a moment.' The smile that came to his lips as he said this faded fast. He went on to say, 'Argyro looked at me as if I was mad but I explained that the property would then be hers and she would be married just as her baba had always intended. Everything in her world would be well, and she would have her dowry after all.'

Vasso flinched and then checked to make sure her involuntary reaction had not disturbed the baby.

'I thought what I was doing was a kindness, but now I wonder if it was wrong and cruel, and I think Argyro feels that, too.'

'It was probably not the best reason.' Vasso tried to think of kind things to say. 'But people have been married for worse ones... Some in our village have been married for land. I knew a girl who was married to end a feud between two families.'

'I know, but those are people who try to make their marriages work.'

'Oh, come on, Stamatis. You have the patience of a saint. No one could accuse you of not trying to make your marriage work.'

'Ah, but what is the one thing Argyro wants?' Vasso looked up, at these words, as Stamati's hand flew to his mouth. He looked down at his grandchild, and mumbled, 'I'm sorry my dear, I should not have said that. Vasso followed his gaze to the child, and wondered if she understood his meaning. 'Well, I have said it now,' he continued after a long pause, 'and you may as well know. The fact is, that is the one act I cannot bring myself to do. It never occurred to me before we were married. Not only was I consumed by my grief but I still felt very married to Anna. Hard as it might be to believe it, it was something that had not occurred to me, I had blocked the thought from my mind entirely. As time has passed, I've realised that as long as I love Anna I cannot go near Argyro, and...' He sighed and his shoulders dropped. 'I will always love Anna.'

'Does Spiros know all this?' Vasso asked.

'No. And I do not want him to know.' A look of fear crossed his face. 'It would humiliate Argyro even more if anyone knew, and it would make me a fool in my child's eyes.' He hesitated. 'I am sorry, Vasso – I had not meant to be so indiscreet. I have burdened you, and I did not mean to do that.' Vasso shook her head, trying to reassure the old man. 'I guess some things are easier to tell to someone who is not so involved. Is it possible that this could be our secret, Vasso? Please say you will not tell him.'

'Under any other circumstances I would not keep a secret from Spiros – but this one? I think it would hurt him more to know it than for me to keep it.'

'Thank you, Vasso. And do you see me with different eyes, now you know how cruel I have been?'

'I can see why you put up with so much from her, but you did what you did at a time when you were very distressed. If it had been me that was asked by a man who was grieving I would have told him to ask again in a year. All the blame cannot be on your shoulders. Argyro was very quick to grab what she thought should be hers, is all I can say.'

'Vasso, you are a kind-hearted woman. Spiros has chosen someone like his mama and I am proud of him.'

'Well, I think I have my answer as to whether I can call this little one Theodoris. But I warn you, Spiros said he was going to use this as a way to ask you about his papous. He knows there is something so you might want to think what you intend telling him.'

'What shall I tell him, Vasso? What would you do?' The white showed all around his irises, one fist grinding into his other palm, his legs twitching.

'I cannot tell you that, Stamatis. I have no idea what I would say. I suspect if he knew about this, what little relationship he has with Argyro would just sink to nothing. He would lose any respect he has for her.'

'And for me.' Stamatis hung his head.

'The difference is he loves you.'

Chapter 33

'How's your day going?' Spiros returned late one morning to check on Vasso and the little one. He cooed and admired the baby all over again, checking tiny hands and feet, watching his expressions, growing anxious when he cried and looking relieved when he peacefully fed.

'You know what, Spiro? I never knew my baba. He was not a great man by all I've heard, but his baba, my papous, was as soft and as kind a man as you could hope to meet. He supported Mama through my baba's absences before he died, so I have heard. He took her side in arguments, Mama has told me. You know, I think I would like to name our boy after him.'

'What was his name?'

'Thanasis. Do you like it? Although' – she chattered on quickly – 'I'm aware there was a boy at school called Thanasis, and because of his love of donkeys he was always called Donkey Boy, but there is no reason why the two should be linked. I mean, we are here on Orino Island, anyway, not in my village...' She knew she was talking too much but she wanted it to seem that her thoughts about the name were genuine and she wanted to make the point, inside herself at least, that her choice had good reason and had nothing to do with Spiro's papous.

'Thanasis?' He looked at the baby, who was watching the tree outside as it waved against the blue sky. 'It suits him.'

'So we're agreed?' She felt she was being cunning and she did not like the feeling at all. She wanted no secrets, so she reminded herself that her secret was for Spiro's and for Stamati's sake and she held her tongue.

The baby, still known as 'Baby', grew quickly, and soon it was time for the priest to baptise him. Vasso's mama and Stella made the visit to the island again for this great celebration, arriving on the Friday and leaving on the Sunday, and fussing over Thanasis, as he was officially known from then on, all weekend. Argyro had insisted on buying the christening clothes and, after his immersion in oil and water, she took him from Vasso and dried him gently, and dressed him in the lace finery. When she handed him back he was crying in his heavy, starched uniform. It was clear to Vasso that he was uncomfortable and overly hot but it would be an affront to Argyro to remove the garments. Stella, on the other hand, had no such reserve and she removed the frilled collar from his smock, handing it back to Argyro, who seemed too shocked to say anything. Outside the church, Stella continued to peel away layers, handing each in turn to Argyro, who appeared to have met her match. Stamatis drank wine, in moderation, and sat slumped in a chair repeating the name Thanasis over and over again to himself. Hearing it on his lips, Vasso began to love the name as she loved the child and it no longer felt important that she had a secret with Stamatis.

Up to this point, Spiros had tried not to pressure her to return to work, but shortly after the baptism he came home one day after a long shift, exhausted.

'I'm not sure how much longer I can stand her. All these promises of letting me order the produce, of putting the place in my name... I no longer believe her. I'm just a wage earner and all the skills I have are making the profit for her, that grumbling, argumentative old hag.'

'Keep your voice down! You'll wake Thanasis.' Vasso sat behind him on the bed and rubbed his shoulders.

'Do you think you could come back to work for at least one shift a day, Vasso? Just so I can have some peace and gain some perspective?'

'My poor Spiros. Is she really so bad? You said she had quietened down.'

'Have you forgotten what she is like? And she is ruder to Baba than ever. I swear she's been worse to him since Thanasis arrived. Sometimes I feel I'm on the brink of slapping her!'

Through the window Vasso could see the closed shutters of Argyro's bedroom. Thanasis must be a daily reminder to her of her situation. She had neither a child not a loving, close relationship. Apart from anything else, she must feel so very alone.

'Don't be too harsh, Spiro.'

'Harsh? You are calling me harsh? Vasso, I can't stand it any more and you accuse me of being harsh.'

'Shh, my love.'

'Come Vasso, do the evening shift, when he is asleep. Argyro can watch him when he sleeps.'

She looked at their sleeping child for a while, listening to his breathing, thinking.

'Okay, I will try an evening shift to see how it goes, but Thanasis comes with me – and *Argyro – stays – at – home*.' She pronounced the last four words individually to make her point.

'And you call me harsh?' He allowed his shoulders to relax, and there was a teasing tone in his voice. 'So, can we try it tomorrow?' The energy in his voice showed his enthusiasm.

'Sure, why not.' And she leaned over his shoulder to kiss him.

Taking Thanasis to the taverna did not seem to be a problem. He slept most of the evening and needed very little attention, and so it was agreed that she would go in every other night. Soon she was working every night, and still the arrangement worked well. But as the weeks turned to months the child slept less and he was determined to crawl everywhere he could and put everything he could find into his mouth. At first, Vasso put a blanket down for him so his little knees would not be scuffed on the flagged floor, but he soon pushed past the limits of the softness. Then he became faster and Vasso found she could hardly turn her back to wash a plate without him getting to the taverna door or picking something off the floor and cramming it in his mouth.

'No, dangerous!' Vasso heard Argyro say, and she turned to find her mother-in-law taking a butter knife from his tiny, tight grip. Spiros, typically, was oblivious as he worked away behind the grill and Stamatis was out serving people, and for once Vasso felt grateful for Argyro's presence. But then Argyro opened her mouth and the feeling died away. 'If you cannot keep him safe he should not be here,' she snapped, and before Vasso could answer Argyro was walking away muttering, with the child in her arms.

Vasso became ever more vigilant but she began to doubt herself when Argyro saved little Thanasis a second time after he found a piece of broken glass, and a third time when she found him playing with a mousetrap. Although the mousetrap was not set, and therefore unlikely to harm his little fingers, it was what made Vasso suspicious, because the traps were always by the back door in the courtyard, a place Thanasis could not go. She mentioned her concern to Spiros one evening but he dismissed her claims as paranoid, kissed her on the top of her head and went off to shower.

The customers, of course, loved Thanasis and they passed him from one to another, pinching his cheeks, encouraging him to walk. So, although Vasso was still haunted by her concerns about his safety and distrust of Argyro, she delighted in watching her son flourish from all the positive attention he got when she was at work, and she held herself in check, sharing her concerns with no one.

Then he discovered the area behind the counter where his baba worked. The flames of the stove mesmerised him, and his little hands grabbed for the knives that flashed as his baba chopped rapidly. These implements were razor sharp, unlike the earlier butter knife, and soon what had been a case of keeping an eye on him became a continuous nervous exercise and the possibility of serious harm coming to him became ever greater as he grew. The incidents of the knife, the broken glass and the mousetrap faded into insignificance beside the harm that could come to him if he went behind the grill.

Of course, the inevitable happened, one day when everybody was distracted for a second. The fat spat. Thanasis shrieked. Stamati's tray crashed to the floor outside as he came running. Vasso dropped a glass in the sink, leaving the smashed pieces as she leapt to the child's side. Spiros left the chicken to burn as he crouched down to grab his son. But the first person to reach him was Argyro, her arm around him, pulling him into her chest, rocking him, making soothing noises. She did not let him go when Vasso reached him, nor when Spiro's hand was on her shoulder.

'Argyro, let us see, let us see how he is hurt.' Stamatis tried to separate them. 'Argyro!' he insisted and reluctantly she made a space between her chest and the child, but not enough for anyone to see what had happened.

'I think it must have been the fat spitting. Argyro we need to run cool water on it, please let us see.' But still the woman held fast.

Vasso gripped Argyro's forearm and physically pulled it away from Thanasis. Finally Argyro relented and Vasso pushed her to one side.

It was only a small burn but it was enough. Vasso scooped him into her arms and was away out of the taverna before anyone could stop her.

'Let her go, Spiro. The boy is not badly hurt. Let them be together.' Stamati's final words came with a flash of warning to Argyro.

Flames leapt from the grill, the smoke billowing up to the roof.

'The chicken!' Spiros screamed and he ran to save the flaming mess.

Chapter 34

'Why are you home so early?' Vasso asked.

'I burnt the chicken,' Spiros growled.

'How do you mean?'

'I mean I burnt the food!' he pulled off his shirt.

'You never burn food.'

'Well, today I burnt the food.' He peered at Thanasis, who lay on his back, arms outstretched, fast asleep.

'He's fine,' Vasso assured him. 'So how come you burnt the food?'

'Him,' he said, an accusing finger pointed at Thanasis. 'I burnt the chicken when he was hurt, and with the rest of what I have cooked I could not have done a worse job because my mind was on him, because you are not looking after him.' He went through to the tiny bathroom. The water hissed from the shower head. He would not be able to hear her now so

271

Vasso said nothing. She waited till he came back in with a towel around his waist, his hair wet.

'Are you saying it is Thanasi's fault?' She would not have Thanasis accused of something that was clearly Spiro's oversight. 'If you had kept your eye on him…'

'So I have to cook and mind the child now?' He made no effort to keep his voice lowered, which inflamed Vasso even more.

'Keep your voice down!' But her voice was as loud as his. Her heart beat fast and anger surged up though her chest and she felt ready to explode. It felt like she was alone in caring for Thanasis, and yet she must go into the taverna and work as she had always done, to make Spiro's life easier. Not only that but, as she recalled the incidents with the mousetrap, the knife and the broken glass, the more she wondered about Argyro. Could it be possible that the woman would put her son in harm's way in order to prove that Vasso was a bad mama? And Spiros would hear none of it! He wanted everything peaceful, smooth and easy, so he could concentrate on his work. Well, if she was the only person looking out for Thanasis she would do it on her own terms and that would not be at the taverna. Spiros would have to work with Argyro.

'*You* keep your voice down. You are quick to tell *me!*' Spiros retorted.

272

'Shhhh.' Vasso tried not to retaliate.

'To hell with your shhh. If you had done your job of minding him back in the taverna tonight's food would not be ruined.'

'I am sure it was not ruined.' Vasso looked up at Spiros as he stood over her. She lay on the bed, her head on her hand as she rested on one elbow, half curled around Thanasis, trying her best to stay relaxed.

'You cannot have him at the taverna any more.' He did not seem to care that he would wake Thanasis with the volume of his voice. 'He must stay here, and Argyro will look after him.' His anger only increased as he spoke and Vasso felt adrenaline course through her in response. 'I have a kitchen to run, that is my priority. I will not debate this point.' By the end of his speech he was more furious than she had ever seen him, and Vasso wondered if Argyro had added fuel to this fire. But, whatever had happened, she was not going to be told what to do with Thanasis. Not even by her husband.

'So it is only you who decides, is it? So your kitchen is more important than our son? Did I not say this before we were married? You should never have married me, Spiro, if you are always going to put your work first.'

'Of course I put my work first! How else am I going to provide for you?'

'That is a good excuse, but the truth is that your cooking has always come first, and everything is just used as an excuse to hide that fact.'

'You used to be supportive of my cooking. I will not be moved on this point, Vasso. Thanasis does not come into the taverna any more, and nor does Argyro. She can stay at home and look after him.'

'So now you are telling me, not discussing things with me? Well, I do not work like that, Spiro. If you wanted someone meek, you should have married someone weak.'

'You pretended to be sweet when I married you.'

That hit Vasso hard. How dare he!

'Since then I have had to put up with you and Argyro arguing,' she countered, her head off her hand now as she sat up, the adrenaline coursing through her in waves. 'And when Thanasis gets burnt you blame your shortcomings on our son.' Her hands made fists, the baby stirred. 'Sometimes I wonder if Argyro is not just an excuse for your single-minded bad temper. Someone to blame if things go wrong.' She knew she was being unreasonable but she wanted to hurt him for even suggesting she had tricked him into marriage. Spiros was no more bad-tempered than his baba by nature. Single-minded perhaps, selfish even, but not bad-tempered. But poor Thanasis could have been badly hurt and Spiros did not seem to feel that this was the most important point. It felt terrifying, as if, out of nowhere, her marriage had become a mistake. Her whole world suddenly seemed like it was on an unsure footing. But lashing out at the person she loved most was not an answer, and as quickly as her anger had erupted she repented.

'Sorry.' She quickly retracted her words. But he was pulling back on his trousers and, grabbing a T-shirt, he left, the door slamming, but not shutting, behind him. Thanasis awoke and began to cry.

Vasso burst into tears and condemned herself for every word she had said as she lifted her charge and began to rock him back to sleep. Outside, below the window, Spiro's footsteps rang out as he marched across the courtyard, his boots heavy against the flags.

'Spiro!' Argyro's voice rose from the direction of the main house.

'What do you want?' Spiros spat.

'A solution.' Argyro sounded calm, calculating.

275

Sniffing hard to stop herself crying, and rocking Thanasis quite roughly, which he sometimes seemed to like, she waited to hear Spiro's reply.

He made none.

'I have a solution,' Argyro said, and Vasso heard the door of Stamati's and Argyro's house open. Then came the sound of papers being shuffled, presumably on the kitchen table. 'These are the legal papers to the taverna.'

Vasso moved to the window. What was Argyro plotting? She hoped for once this was something good, something positive, but more likely it was just some new way Argyro had found of wielding her power. The open door threw a rectangle of orange light across the courtyard. The distance was short, but from one storey up she could not see them now they were inside. She put the now-sleeping Thanasis back on the bed and leaned out of the window.

'I have been to a lawyer,' Argyro said with authority. 'These papers put the taverna into your name, if we sign – here and here.' Vasso hand covered her mouth, stopping her sharp intake of breath. The papers rustled. What was Argyro up to? Did Stamatis know? Why would she give over the taverna to Spiros? She could imagine Spiros reading the papers, checking them over, trying to make out if they were real, what they were really about.

'No catch,' Spiro's stepmother said. Vasso did not believe her.

'Please do not do anything rash just because we have argued, Spiro,' she muttered to herself, willing him to stay calm.

'In return I want two things.' Ah – here it came. With Argyro there was never something for nothing. This would be the catch and Spiros would come storming out, calling her names, another argument. She braced herself, looked back at Thanasis to see if he was sleeping soundly. All this arguing around him could not be healthy.

'Name them.' Spiro's voice sounded cautious but ready for a fight. Vasso was so sick of the loud words, the tension, the accusations thrown from Argyro to, it seemed, any member of her family who was close enough, that she willed this to really be a solution.

'Stamatis keeps his job, always,' Argyro stated, and waited for Spiros to say something.

'Why would I not want him working?' Spiros sounded puzzled.

'And…'

The leaves of the grapevine that grew up the side of Stamati's house rustled on the slight breeze and Vasso leaned even further out of the window so as not to miss what was being said.

'The child is mine to bring up.'

Vasso wondered if she had misheard. She replayed the sounds in her head. Was she mistaken?

'If you sign here... and here... than I become his official warden.'

Every muscle and fibre in Vasso stiffened and the familiar swirling of the world that preceded her faints made her pull her head in from the window so she could grip the back of a chair. She must compose herself, go down and support Spiros. His anger would know no bounds. Might he even become violent? No. That was not who he was. But she must go to him, support him, show their solidarity.

The swirling in her head settled and, as it did, she took another look out of the window. Spiro's fingers were round the edge of the door, and as she watched he closed it, with him and Argyro, and the papers that could sign her son over to the old witch, on the inside.

Chapter 35

'You know, Juliet, I would quite enjoy a glass of wine.' Vasso stretches out her arms and legs. The tops of her little fingers are beginning to curve inward and the veins show, raised, on the back of her hands. But aging has been mostly kind to her. There are no serious aches or pains and she has no complaints.

'You can't leave the story there!' Juliet says, sitting up in the hammock. The cat that was curled on her lap jumps down, leans back against its front legs, tail high in the air, and yawns.

'Also, I am getting eaten alive.' Vasso runs a hand down the back of her legs, feeling at the bumps, trying not to scratch. Juliet is already on her feet. She lights a citrus candle and puts it on the floor between them.

'Red or white?'

'Oh, red. With ice,' Vasso calls, watching Juliet disappear inside. She lifts her arms to allow the air to circulate. The evening is so still that the slight drop in temperature now the sun has gone is almost imperceptible.

Would she have had the same reaction if the situation with Argyro and Spiros happened today? Of course she wouldn't, she is older and wiser. But back then it all seemed so raw and immediate. And she has never, not once, regretted what she did. In fact, it was the best move she could have made – not that she was aware of that at the time. But as for being that age again – no way! Not for straight fingers, smooth hands and a face free of lines. It was all far too painful.

'So, tell me.' Juliet returns with a tall glass of red wine for each of them, ice clinking against the side. 'Do you want anything to eat, by the way?' she asks before lowering herself back into her hammock. Vasso tuts a typical Greek no. She is not hungry quite yet.

'So, go on, what happened?'

'Ah well, I was young and spirited and as I watched the door close a few things came to mind.' It seems so long ago now, almost like it was a dream or a film she once saw. 'I remember I had caught Argyro trying to teach Thanasis the word "mama" one day when she thought I was stuck with a customer and Spiros was banging and clattering in the kitchen.' So long ago and yet the pain, the hurt, is still there, as if it was yesterday. 'Only, when she said the word "mama", she pointed to herself, patted herself on the chest... and another time when she was telling him that if he ever needed anything he must go to her first.' She makes a concerted effort to not let the anger grow in her again. She has worked through it, forgiven Argyro, and come to terms with it. There is nothing to be gained in igniting all that emotion again. She breathes deeply, slowly. 'He was too small to understand her words but I could see what her intention was – and all this rushed to the forefront of my mind.'

'Right, so what happened?' Juliet does not sit back in her chair. Instead she shuffles her feet and rocks her glass back and forth, making the ice tinkle.

'Well, I looked at Thanasis and I realised he was my priority. He came first. He came before Argyro, before Spiros. Even before me. But it went further. He was more important than my mama, than the public's opinion of me, than everything.'

The intensity of that moment returns to her as if it had happened last week, not thirty-five years ago. There had been no decision, no struggle to make up her mind what to do; she just did it. She lifted Thanasis from the bed, took what little money Spiros had stashed in a tear in the mattress, and with nothing but this and the clothes she stood up in, and a few nappies, pressing Thanasis to her breast so he would not wake up, she pattered downstairs, out of the courtyard and along the passage to the port.

It was late enough and fairly quiet. She passed a man whom she had served at the taverna a few days before, and he nodded but neither of them spoke. Her legs were propelling her but she had no idea where she was going. The place that she felt drawn to was the church next to the windmill. But, though Thanasis was only small and would probably never remember it if they were to sleep on the church steps or by the windmill, that was not the life she wanted to give him, living like the gypsies who slept under the pine trees in Saros town – not even for one night, not if she could help it. She stopped under the single street light that lifted the cobbles into high relief and counted the money.

At the port's corner, the dull glow of an oil lamp shone as it swung in the hand of a local fisherman who was standing on shore. Down in the water, his legs splayed and his knees bent to compensate for the rocking of his small boat, was another man who did not look Greek. The boat's name glowed in the light: *TT Irida*. Vasso knew that 'TT' meant 'tender to', and that this small boat would be used by the foreigner to get to his yacht, which would be anchored offshore somewhere.

'You can never tell,' the fisherman said. 'Some nights can be lucky, and you can catch lots of fish. Some aren't.' He ambled his way up one of the side streets and disappeared into the shadows.

'Ah, but it's nice, no? To sit in a boat under the moon, fish or no fish. Goodnight, my friend,' the other called into the darkness, in a thick accent, and then set about pulling on ropes, releasing himself from the harbour.

'Excuse me.' Vasso walked right up to the harbour's edge. 'Are you going to the mainland?' This was devious; she knew he would not be. He would likely only be going as far as his yacht, at this time of night.

'Oh my dear, is that a baby you have there? Why are you out so late?

And another lie rolled from her tongue.

'I have word that my mama is ill, and I must go to her.'

He looked over his shoulder, across to the mainland. 'Is she just across there?' he asked, his work with the ropes paused.

'No, just outside Saros. But over there will do.'

'Saros, ok. I am going, tomorrow... er... But tonight is ok too.' He scratched his head and frowned at her, but soon smiled again. 'Yes,' he continued, 'come, we will go!' He smiled and held out his hand to help her onto the gently rocking boat and showed her where to sit before pulling the cord to start the outboard motor.

Vasso held Thanasis close and pulled her shawl over him to stop the wind disturbing his sleep. In the dark of the bay a shape loomed black, pinpoints of light dotted along its side. They motored on and the shape grew and grew. Surely only a king could own such a large vessel!

Lights came on as they got nearer, and half a dozen uniformed Asians came running out to help them on board. Everything was shiny and new and the brightness of it all dazzled her. She was helped onboard by one of the crew, whose nails were manicured and uniform spotlessly white. The stern area was covered by an upper deck but open to the warm night air on three sides. In the centre was a large polished wooden table with seating for ten or so, and yet the space was larger than the whole of Stamati's taverna. Glasses and plates and silver cutlery were laid out neatly on the wood. Linen napkins fanned in pleats in tall-stemmed wine glasses. It was like a picture from one of Vasso's magazines, and she could not stop staring at the beauty of it all.

'Any luck, darling?' a lazy voice said in English, which immediately made Vasso feel like she was in a film. 'Oh, what have we here?' A woman in a long, flowing gown came through sliding doors, a glass in her hand, rings adorning long fingers.

'Crystal this is... Sorry my dear, I do not know your name.' Vasso looked at him blankly and he repeated himself in clumsy Greek.

Introductions were made; Vasso tried to get her tongue to say the woman's name but it did not seem right to be so informal having only just met her, and she addressed her as Kyria Crystal, which made the woman lift her chin and lengthen her neck. The look she gave her made Vasso feel small and she clutched Thanasis more tightly.

'Well, Vasso, and who is this?' Crystal asked in broken Greek, and she stepped closer and pulled away the shawl to see Thanasi's reposeful face. 'Oh-so small. Christopher, do you remember when Gabrielle was so small?'

'You have no objections to sailing tonight, do you?' he asked. She did not answer and the man gave commands to his crew to raise the anchor and set sail for Saros.

Vasso yawned. It was late and all the emotions of the evening had also drained her energy.

'Would you like a gin and tonic before you go to bed?' Crystal did not wait for an answer. 'You can have the yellow guest room.'

And she turned and gave instructions in English to a uniformed girl who had been silently standing by the sliding doors. The girl looked at Vasso and appeared to be waiting.

'Well, goodnight,' Crystal said dismissively.

Vasso could not even manage a goodnight. As the sliding door was pushed back for her to enter she could not help but stare at the huge flower display on the table in the lounge being opened to her. The table itself shone so deeply that it reflected the ceiling, itself all polished metal. The portholes were so large that Vasso would have called them windows, and they were draped with evenly pleated swags of material. Lamps in the same fabric stood on every surface casting a subdued light, and it smelt of jasmine, but somehow not real jasmine – rather, a simulation of the real thing.

'Goodnight, Vasso,' Christopher called from outside where he was busy helping one of the crew secure the tender to the back of the boat.

'*Kalinixta*,' Vasso managed and before she could take in any more of the room she obediently followed the uniformed woman who was disappearing down a hallway at the far end. As she left, she heard Crystal say something in English to Christopher in a tone that suggested annoyance, and Christopher's reply was calm and patient. Crystal's tone changed to something grating and high-pitched. She spat out the words in her foreign tongue and Christopher replied meekly. Vasso sighed. Even here, with all this wealth and beauty, it was possible to be discontented. Would Argyro be any happier in such a position? Argyro would think so, but Vasso wondered if people chose the circumstances they tolerated just to prove – exaggerate, even – how imperfect their lot was in the world. If she had stayed on Orino she would have had plenty of reason to complain. But she had not stayed. She had faced her problem straight on and made a change before the situation became unbearable. Maybe this is what Argyro should do, and Crystal perhaps? But then, without really knowing anything about Crystal, she could guess that this graceful foreign woman would no more let go of her wealth than Argyro would the taverna, even to be happy.

'Being unhappy in order to feel wealthy is madness.' She didn't intend to say this out loud. The Asian woman turned and smiled.

'Do you speak Greek?' Vasso asked. The corridor, with its deep-pile carpet, seemed to be going on forever. The woman did not reply but she stopped outside a door, pushed it open and, with an outstretched arm, invited Vasso to enter.

287

In the room, two lamps on the table by the far wall each lit a single bed. The covers were a pale lemon yellow and they matched more swags of material hanging at the windows. Everything looked new and untouched. She looked behind her as the door was closed to see a lemon-yellow bathrobe hanging on the back of the door. It was as cool as spring in that overly draped cabin. She opened the door of what she thought might be a wardrobe, and it turned out to be a bathroom. Another door revealed a wardrobe so big she could walk into it. A long mirror was attached to the wall at the far end and everywhere the carpet was so thick her feet sank into it.

'Oh my, Thanasis, I wish you were old enough that you would remember this!' After laying him carefully on one of the single beds, Vasso could not resist the temptation to have a shower, just because it was all so grand. She slipped off her clothes, but did not put on the bathrobe in case it belonged to someone and they had just forgotten it. The glass-walled shower was huge. Vasso turned on the tap and stood to one side, testing the temperature, but the water was immediately warm, and the temperature stayed steady with no need to adjust the cold tap. She climbed in and turned around and around, letting the flow of warm water soothe her, trying to ignore the fact that she had just left her husband. On a glass shelf were soap, shampoo and something labelled as shampoo cream. She was not totally sure if she should use them – but then, why not? If a guest came to stay at her house she would make all these things available to them if she had them.

She washed with the soap and used the shampoo, and then, just because it was there, she used the shampoo cream, and her hair became soft and silky like she had never felt it before. The hot water did not run out and she only left the luxury of it behind when she thought she heard Thanasis stir.

The towel was so big it went round her twice and, once it was safely tucked in, and she had checked on her child, who seemed to be sleeping well with the gentle movement of the boat, she set about cleaning the shower so it looked new again. Then, even though she was tired and the bed looked tempting, she found she could not sleep just yet as she had discovered a bottle of body lotion, some hand cream and a hairdryer on the dressing table. A small part of her knew that this care she was lavishing on herself was her response to the fact that she was now on her own. There was no one but herself to take care of her.

A tap at the door startled her, and she opened it cautiously. Another Asian lady stood there, bowing slightly, and holding out a folded bundle that turned out to be satin pyjamas.

The novelty and luxury of the moment was not only distracting her from her plight, but also heightened her awareness of how little care she had taken of herself in recent months – certainly since Thanasis was born. This realisation seemed to release something within her, a tension that she had perhaps been holding unnoticed; consequently, when she lay down it was as if a weight had been lifted from her, and she slept soundly.

The next morning she was woken by another tap on her door and presented with coffee and toast with butter and a choice of marmalades on a tray.

Thanasis awoke as Vasso was taking her first sip of coffee and without a word the Asian lady picked him up, made a soft murmuring sound and rocked him gently. Vasso was about to intervene when she saw the look on the woman's face. She was in bliss and a tear ran down her cheek.

Vasso put her hand on the woman's shoulder, and she looked up and smiled through her tears. She pointed to Thanasis, then to herself, and then in a big arch towards the window, out into the distance. With her free hand she held up five fingers and then held her hand above the floor at about Thanasi's height, then two inches higher, then higher still until the fifth time her hand was level with her shoulder.

The woman walked with Thanasis to the window, and Vasso sat back down and ate her breakfast. Just as she was finishing, there was another tap on the door. The Asian woman's look of bliss was replaced with one of fear, and she hastily handed Thanasis back and took the tray from Vasso's knee.

It was Christopher, who came in, smiling.

'You slept well? We are in Saros. Crystal and I, we go now, for coffee.' He held out his hand. 'It was a pleasure to meet you and I wish your mama that her illness passes.' Vasso smiled at his clumsy Greek and shook his proffered hand, muttering a hundred thank-yous, in Greek and English, which made Christopher smile again. The maid slipped out past him, and then he left and she was alone with Thanasis.

She made the bed and put everything straight, and took one last look, trying to memorise the details. She let herself out into the corridor and found the way by which she had entered.

The crew, who were busy polishing everything in sight, ignored her, which felt

291

stranger than the false courtesy that they had displayed the night before.

Saros seemed almost alien after her long absence, as if she had never left and, at the same time, as if she had been away for much longer than two years.

Two years gone, and she was married and separated with a one-year-old child. Mama would be far from happy.

She set out on the coastal track towards the village, keen to avoid the main roads, and anxious to get home unseen so she could be the first to explain the situation to her mama.

Chapter 36

The village seemed so familiar. The slight sense of isolation she had felt, even in the height of her love with Spiros, dropped away as if it had never been there. Looking over the burnt-orange tiled roofs she could name the people who lived in every one. Each with a connection to her – a second aunt, a cousin, a school friend. Each always found a place at their table for her if she ever dropped round, and each treated her like family. Why didn't Argyro have that on the island? What a life she had created for herself with her moaning and resentment!

Vasso spotted the roof of her own house, tucked away just down the path opposite the church. Noting the cross atop the dome of the church, she reflected that her mama was sure to make her see the priest, and he might press her to return to her husband. She puffed out a big breath through inflated cheeks. The whole village would gossip, for a while at least.

Everyone with their own opinions, many condemning of her, especially those of the older generation.

Or would they? Surely once they knew Argyro wanted to take her son they would not expect her to be reunited with Spiros? She could not imagine her mama signing away her only grandchild, nor the priest suggesting that she go back to such a situation. Who in the village would think such a thing was acceptable? No one! Not even Maria, her nearest neighbour by the church, and she was really not fond of children.

The village harbour seemed more decayed and unused than ever, but three small fishing boats were tied up there. She knew who owned each one.

The track to the village was clear, marked by goat-trimmed bushes and eaten-away grass. If she went up to the left she could cut through the orange orchard and come up behind her house.

The first house she came to, right at the end of her lane, had a hand-written sign on the gate which read *TO LET*. It had been empty as long as she could remember. A cat lounged on the terrace as if it owned the place. The drive was swept clean of leaves, and the garden was neatly tended.

Washing hung heavily in the garden at the side of her house, as if it was still wet. Mama must have hung it out within the last half hour.

Thanasis murmured. Vasso's arms were exhausted from carrying him, and as she shifted him over to the other side he awoke.

'Nearly there, my little doll,' she told him. There was a slight pounding in her ears, the sound of her heart racing, but she told herself that she was being foolish. No one would condemn her for what she had done, would they?

At her own back door she paused and wondered if she should knock. She did not want to scare her mama.

'Mama?' she called instead.

'You know, I think I'm starting to get a little hungry now,' Vasso remarks to Juliet, pausing her tale.

'You, Vasso my friend, are a tease.' Juliet laughs and, lurching forward, she disentangles herself from her hammock seat to take the glasses indoors. She returns with them full, and the bottle tucked under one arm.

'I cannot drink another glass on an empty stomach!'

'I've nothing cooked...'

'Let's go to Stella's.'

'If I keep eating at Stella's I'm going to be round as a barrel.' Juliet rubs one thin foot over the other and slips on her flip-flops. 'But you've talked me into it!' She manages to stand, this time with slightly more elegance, and the chair swings unburdened behind her.

'Put the wine in the fridge,' Vasso says, offering her glass back, and then pats her hair to give it more shape.

Juliet leaves the door unlocked and the gate open. They wander side by side down the lane and out towards the village square. It's late enough now that the air is slightly cooler, and this has brought life to the village. Children play by the kiosk, run between the chairs and tables that have been taken out of the *kafeneio*. The older men sit and watch the news and football scores on the television that has been propped in the window, facing out for all to see.

'Look.' Vasso points to a carrier bag of beer bottles resting by one of the fridges in the kiosk – empties that have been returned by a customer but not stacked neatly in the crates round the back. 'That is what happens when you employ someone. They do not care as they would if it were their own.' The kiosk is a wooden box painted mustard yellow with a shelf all the way around the outside at elbow height, and a window on each side. The shelf itself bows under the weight of boxes of sweets, plastic cigarette lighters standing sentinel in containers, packs of cards, hanging plastic *komboloi* – worry beads – and endless piles of other daily essentials in multiples. Over the years, Vasso has added a line of drink coolers down one side, a magazine rack down the other, a freezer chest of ice creams in the middle. Her emporium has grown and now she sells everything but fresh food. She leaves that to Marina at the corner shop.

'Costa did you know there was a bag of bottles just dumped by that end fridge?'

She addresses the man in the box, who tears his eyes reluctantly away from his phone. It beeps at him and he glances back at it; he looks disappointed, then pockets the item and turns his attention to Vasso.

'What?'

Vasso points, and Costa slides reluctantly from his chair, taking his time to come out of the back of the kiosk and around it to see what she is indicating.

'Oh, yes, right.' He picks up the bag and takes it round the back, where he laboriously transfers the bottles into one of the crates.

'How long have you had the kiosk?' Juliet asks. 'No, wait, you were telling me that you just got back from Orino Island with Thanasis. How is he, by the way?'

'He's very well, and I have some news for you. But first, let us eat.' Vasso waves to Stella across the road.

Stella's eatery is just beyond the square. It has half a dozen tables and chairs outside, arranged around a tree that has been wound round with fairy lights. There are two doors from the street: a narrow one into the dining area with its rough wooden tables, that the farmers tend to dominate, and a wide double door that puts the counter in front of the grill almost on the street, making it easy to serve the takeaways. The tables and chairs out on the pavement are a relatively new addition to tempt lazy housewives and their children, and to snag the occasional tourist.

'Hello, you two,' Stella greets them. She has on one of her usual sleeveless floral print dresses. This one, a size too large, is loosely belted to give it some shape and accentuates her small frame. Vasso is well aware her old school friend looks years younger than her. Her shoulder-length hair is loose, which gives the impression of ease, but it is her animation, her energy, that defies the years.

'Are you here to eat or chat?' Stella pulls out a chair as if ready to sit with them.

'Eat!' Vasso declares.

'Well, the chicken's cooked, the sausages are just done, the chips are fresh and the usual other things are all…' She absently waves her hand towards the grill, as they know well what is available.

'I'll just have a salad,' Juliet says. 'And maybe just a few chips.' She sits. 'Oh, and a beer.'

'Chicken and lemon sauce.' Vasso chooses a chair.

'And some *tzatziki*,' Juliet adds.

Stella waits.

'Actually, I might have some chicken, too. With lemon sauce, please,' Juliet relents, and Stella goes inside. 'So, come on, you were at the back door calling your mama.'

'To be honest, Juliet, there is not much more to tell. My mama was glad to see me of course, and I think even more glad to see Thanasis. When she heard what Spiros had done she could not believe it. In fact she *did* not believe it. She believed that Argyro might have made the offer but I had to convince her of Spiro's part.'

'Are you talking about Spiros?' Stella comes out with two plates full of food. Following her is her husband, Mitsos. He brings three glasses and then returns inside and reappears with a jug of local wine.

'Here you go, girls,' he says, which makes Vasso giggle. 'Sit with your friends, Stella – there are only one or two farmers in tonight.' Mitsos goes back inside.

'He's so good to you,' Vasso says.

'Have you told Juliet about Spiros yet?' Stella asks.

'No, she hasn't. She's being a real tease over this.' Juliet's mouth is full of chips. She pours the wine.

'He was an absolute hero, that Spiros,' Stella says. 'How long were you here, Vasso – four days?'

'Three days.' Vasso is amused that Stella has so much enthusiasm for the tale. She decides to stay quiet and hear her tell it.

'Three days! That's all it took for him to find her. He looked all over Orino Island, asking everyone, but no one had seen her or the child. Then one of the customers said he had seen her late one night, the night she disappeared, down by the port. None of the fishermen admitted giving her a lift off the island and then one of the old boys mentioned a man with a big yacht, a foreigner.'

'I suppose once he knew you were off the island it would be obvious that you would come here.' Juliet scoops *tzatziki* with a hunk of bread.

300

'Spiros pressured a fisherman to take him across to the mainland and then he got rides from people all the way here.' Stella sips her wine, legs stretched out, ankles crossed down the side of the table. 'But he hadn't come to take you back, had he?'

'Oh, you're joking! Had he come only for the child?' Juliet stops eating to look at Vasso.

'He came,' Vasso says, putting down her fork. 'Found me, and do you know what his first words were? "Why?" That's what he said, "Why?" Well, I almost exploded. I called him all the names under the sun and he waited and listened and, when I had exhausted myself, he put his arms on either side of my shoulders, wrapped them around my back and pulled me to him.

'"Vasso," he said, "I don't know if I should be angry or laugh." I pulled away and told him to leave.'

'But really, Vasso,' Stella breaks in. 'How could you actually think he would have signed over Thanasis like that?'

'Don't make me feel a fool all over again,' Vasso warns Stella. 'I felt such a fool, Juliet. Of course he had not agreed anything with Argyro. He had only closed the door so as not to wake his son. He said he had never lost his temper so badly with anyone in all his life. At one point his rage coursed so hot through his veins he thought he might even hit her, but of course he did not.' She turns to Stella. 'There were rumours that Stamatis slapped her across the face. I don't know if they were true. It seems unlikely, though. He is such a sweet-tempered man.'

'Someone should have slapped her,' Juliet interjects. 'I don't think I can eat all these chips. Do you want some, Vasso?'

Vasso helps herself to one or two.

'Stella?'

Stella shakes her head.

'So then what happened? I presume he had to go back to work? And what happened to Argyro and Stamatis?'

'Ah, well...' Vasso says with a smile.

Chapter 37

'It was Spiro's idea, wasn't it?' Stella says.

'No. Well, sort of. I think we decided together. This lemon sauce is a good batch, Stella,' Vasso says.

'Made it this morning. I think the stock was richer than usual.' She leans over the table and takes a spoon from a glass that holds an assortment of cutlery and scoops some sauce from Vasso's plate. 'Yes, not bad. It's one of Spiro's recipes, you know.'

Juliet's eyes widen at the knowledge and she tastes the sauce again.

'So what did you decide together?' Juliet presses.

'To stay here,' Vasso says.

'What, and Spiros left his old taverna just like that?'

'He didn't care. He said he never cared which taverna he worked in, as long as he worked.'

'He got himself a job in a taverna in Saros. As you can imagine, he did well, and after – how long was it, Vasso? – only a year or so, they got their own taverna.' Stella says.

'Oh, I love a happy ever after.' Juliet lifts her glass to chink against her friends' but neither Vasso nor Stella is smiling. 'Oh God, what happened?' She says, putting the glass down.

Vasso cannot speak. It is a day that she has played over in her mind again and again. Spiros had come home so happy, singing as he walked up to their home, through the gate.

'Vasso, my love,' he greeted her as he came into the house. 'If we keep going like this the taverna will be paid off in another two years.' He was so full of life.

'What did they think of your new beef dish?' she asked, closing the door to the room where Thanasis was sleeping.

'They loved it.'

'You work too hard, my love.' She massaged his shoulders as he sat down on the kitchen chair that had been her mama's until the year before, and was now hers. A picture of her mama's face came to her and she put all her tender sorrow into easing the knots out of Spiro's shoulders. She kissed his ear several times as she worked his shoulders and then she kissed his neck.

'These are the days,' Spiros said. 'I must do all I can to make us comfortable now.' And he turned to look at her and kissed her on the mouth. She presumed he was thinking, like her, of the shortness of life, and she understood and kissed him back, impressing the moment into her soul. The kiss grew in passion and Spiros, despite his tiredness, led her by the hand through to their bedroom where he so gently laid her on the bed, and his love flowed in his words and his kisses and his touch and they transcended all that was mortal and floated with the gods until, exhausted, they fell asleep.

In the morning, she was woken as the sun sliced past the edge of the curtain into the room, and rolled over to wrap her arms around him.

'Oh, you are so cold, Spiro,' she exclaimed. But he did not respond. His arms stayed tight across his chest, his legs did not fidget. 'Spiro.' She pushed him playfully. She registered the cold of his skin anew, and it became inhuman, clammy. 'Spiro!' She leaped from the bed, over him, then crouched down beside him to see his face. His eyes were closed but not in peace, his mouth twisted, open, his nose wrinkled. 'Spiro!' she screamed at the top of her voice. It was incomprehensible. 'Spiro!' she screamed again but she knew he could not hear her. 'Spiro!' This time his name emerged as a primal roar, and all that was animal in her rose, and she wailed as if her life was being dragged from her, her soul torn from her body. All her being wanted to be released from her physical body and fly to him, follow him to the other side, but he had gone and she could not follow. 'No! No!' Her tears blurred her vision. The incomprehensible and the impossible were shattering all she knew. Cradling his head, she willed life back into him. She promised the deities anything they wanted if they would give her love breath. Then she cursed them and told them to take her too, but the room remained quiet and still and eventually she sank to the floor, alone.

'Mama?' Thanasis opened the door. How she recovered her control she had no idea, but she was on her feet and over to him in a second, her voice shaky but controlled.

'Baba is a little poorly, Thanasis. Go to your room and play while I get the doctor.' Bless him, he had obeyed, and she had obeyed her own words and she did all she needed to do whilst her soul shrieked for her mate, the part that made her whole, but the sound echoed in the universe and she was left deserted, abandoned.

The words of the woman on Monemvasia came to her, about how, if you are truly loved, you do not feel lonely, and she told the woman through the ether that she could not be more wrong. Vasso was now composed of loneliness, a solitude that was liquid and coursed through her veins. She was just an empty shell, no longer human. She could have borne the pain, the desperation, if Spiros had been there to share it, and the irony hit her and the solitude engulfed her again.

Stamatis and Argyro came to the village and stayed in her house, her mama's house, and she resented Argyro's presence every second. It was easier to be angry at her than at Spiros for leaving her. Stamatis seemed to sink into a familiar place and he pushed Argyro further and further away. Argyro seemed angry but neither Vasso nor Stamatis cared. As time passed, their limbs needed to move even if their minds couldn't, and Vasso and her father-in-law took to going on long walks together. They did not speak, there was nothing to say, but often Stamatis would put his arm over her shoulders, draw her in close and kiss the top of her head. This was as expressive as he got. Vasso, in turn, would lay her head against his shoulder. He knew her pain, having lost his first wife, his true love. As they mourned together, Argyro became ever more excluded, and finally she found some pretext to return to the island, leaving Stamatis to follow a good deal later.

'You see, he knew.' Vasso manages to speak, but she cannot look at Juliet or Stella. 'He had known since just after we were married. That time he had been out of breath, the indigestion, at Monemvasia, had worried him more than he would say and he went to see the doctor. He had the same heart problem as his mama. All the time we were married he had known he would go sooner rather than later, just like his mama, and that is what drove him to work so hard. He wanted to provide for me and Thanasis, so we would be alright after he was…'

Juliet pushes her food away and dabs at her eyes with a napkin.

'He was such a good man,' Stella laments. 'You know, he had taken out life insurance. I had never heard of such a thing at the time!' Both Juliet and Vasso frown a little.

'If he hadn't I have no idea what would have become of me and Thanasis,' Vasso says. Even now, looking back, those days seem confusing, misty.

The lawyer came to see her, and tried to explain, but she did not want to hear. A will seemed so final, somehow, so inhuman. But after Stamatis left Vasso realised that, for Thanasi's sake, she must face the lawyers and try to make some arrangements for the future.

'I am deeply sorry for your loss,' the lawyer began, and Vasso had to grip the arms of the plastic-leather chair to stop herself from standing and leaving the office before any more was said.

'I saw your husband several times.' This caught Vasso's attention. When had he seen Spiros? Why had she not known? 'He was very keen to make sure you and your son were well provided for.' He flipped over some papers in front of him as if scanning for something, before smoothing them flat and trying to look her in the eye. Which he could not.

'He took out some heavy life insurance. I need not bore you with the details, but it is sufficient for you to know that the taverna, as he planned, is now fully paid off. There is also a small lump sum to help you until you find your feet.'

The numbness set into her limbs, and, though she heard his words, all they meant to her was that Spiros was dead. She rose and left, and it was several weeks, maybe even a few months, before she returned and asked him to explain again. During this time she mindlessly went through the motions of life without really being present. Some periods were deeply thoughtful, when she could not command her body to even rise from her bed but the processing in her head would not stop. She thought of Stamati's situation, after Anna died, and understood better how he was not in a place to make good judgments, and she reflected how at the same time, if it was in his power, he would do all he could to ensure that no-one felt as miserable as he did. She could not have considered marrying anyone else , but then no predator like Argyro was there. Maybe if someone had come promising to care of her, and if it were not for the life insurance, things would have been different.

'Without Spiros taking out life insurance I would not have the taverna to lease out and nor could I have bought the kiosk,' Vasso says.

It is heavy and sad to think of these events. Some days, she can think of nothing else, and at these times she has discovered that it's best to talk about something, anything – find something to laugh about, even the silliest, most trivial thing. Right now she has something else to think about that is big, something so good it makes her chuckle just considering it.

'Ah, Juliet,' she says with renewed energy. 'And you too, Stella, I have news for you both! About Thanasis!'

Chapter 38

Stella's mood lifts immediately but Juliet still seems sad.

'I want to hear about your son,' she says, 'but first, what happened to poor Stamatis? He lost his first wife and then he lost his son.'

Vasso leaps up. 'Oh my goodness, they are early,' she cries, and Juliet and Stella look at her wide-eyed, trying to make sense of what is happening.

Vasso, leaving her chair rocking, runs out into the middle of the road and chases a passing taxi into the square, her sturdy heels clipping against the tarmac.

The yellow car comes to a stop by Marina's corner shop and Vasso suppresses her haste and smooths her hair, patting underneath to give it some lift.

The door of the taxi opens and she can hear the chatter of thanks for the lift and the tinkle of coins and then:

'Mama!'

And, just for the moment, in the self-assured way he moves, the fall of his hair and his good looks, she sees Spiros and her heart misses a beat, and then she is in his arms.

'Thanasi, my love, you are early, you said–'

'I'm here!' He kisses her forehead. He is so much taller than her now. His arms engulf her and she breathes in the warm, dark, musky scent that is the same as his baba's and she wants to cry for her loss and cry for the joy of having such a son.

'Ah, Mama, no need to cry! I have brought you a present.' And he releases her to open the back door of the taxi.

'I am seeing things!' she cries. Another Spiros, but an older version, with white hair, the same good looks, the same assurance and easy manner, climbs from the back of the car. She is just as quick to be in this man's arms. His grip is frailer, bonier, but it comes with the same musky scent, which is mixed with something else, as if his clothes have been stored slightly damp. She will wash them for him. She will do everything for him she can.

'Were you not expecting me, Vasso?' Stamatis asks. But Vasso cannot speak for her tears.

'Mama, I hate this to be the first thing I say to you, but I am hungry,' Thanasis says as the taxi leaves. 'First a train, then a bus, then a taxi. It's a long way from Athens.'

'Well, you are in luck. I was sitting at Stella's.' She does not want to let go of Stamatis.

'Does she still make Baba's lemon sauce?'

'She does.' Vasso leads them both, an arm around each.

Outside the kafeneio, Thanasis hugs Stella and everyone is silent at the obviously emotional reunion. Only about a year after Vasso moved home to her mama's house, Stella and her first husband took the house for rent at the end of the lane, and Stella became like a second mama to Thanasis. Not only a second mama but a great friend as well – the sort a real mama cannot be. Vasso knows, without resentment, that Stella holds secrets that Thanasis has told to her that he would have found awkward to share with his own mama. She is so glad that, in his difficult teenage years, Stella was there for him.

'Thanasi, Stamati – this is Juliet. Juliet – Thanasis and Stamatis!' Vasso pulls herself together to make the introductions.

Juliet's eyes are wide. Her mouth opens and closes a few times, which makes Stamatis laugh, and then she shakes Thanasi's hand and pulls him in to kiss him on both cheeks. Stamatis kisses first her hand and then her cheeks, and they are all preparing to sit together when Mitsos, Stella's second husband, comes out and the handshaking and hugging begin again. Then Mitsos goes in to bring plates of food for the new arrivals.

'With Stella's lemon sauce?' Thanasis shouts after him.

Stella pats his knee and gives it a little rub.

'So, Vasso, you dark horse.' Stella cannot sit still in her seat. 'You were expecting them?'

'Of course,' Vasso says, but gives nothing away.

'And is it just a casual drop-by sort of visit?' Stella pushes.

'Not exactly. I did tell you that I have some news, did I not?'

Thanasis puts up his hand to silence everyone.

'Can I just say that I am the most in the dark of anyone? I've come back from my last day in the kitchens. You know the hotel where I was chef is closing, right?' – he addresses no one specifically – 'It was in the wrong location, and was never going to succeed. Well, anyway, when I got home, not only was my suitcase packed but the whole house was empty. I'll be

315

honest, Papou, I was scared. I thought we had been evicted.'

'Would I have been so happy if I'd been evicted?' the old man asks.

Juliet is sitting on her hands on the edge of her chair, looking from one to the other. On first meeting, Juliet appeared elegant, aloof, which amuses Vasso now, because really she is so eager for life, so ready to drink in the world, that she has no time for holding back her emotions.

The dogs around the village have started their evening telegraph of news and the square has grown quiet of children's play. There is just the older generation sitting at the *kafeneio* and outside Stella's eatery now. It is as if they have the village to themselves.

'It runs in the family, then, this teasing nature,' Stella says, and Juliet nods in agreement.

'Stamatis, maybe you should tell Thanasis?' Vasso offers and the old man fidgets as all eyes turn on him. Mitsos brings out the last plate and pulls up a chair.

'Well, several things have happened all at the same time' – he looks at Mitsos as he speaks – 'which made me do some thinking. For one, the people who were renting the taverna on Orino left and so, with a new tenant, I put the rent up.'

Juliet leans towards Stella and whispers, 'What happened to Argyro?' Vasso looks over and smiles and leans across Stella to tell her. 'Ran away with a rich foreigner, who turned out to be both poor and a drunk. They live in a rented flat in Corinth, and she washes floors for a living, apparently.' She pulls a face to express how distasteful she imagines Argyro's new situation to be.

It seems their whispers are far from quiet as Thanasis joins in.

'She got what she deserved. Or maybe she made it happen so she could really have something to moan about.'

'Now, *paidi mou*' – Stamatis addresses Thanasis with the term of endearment – 'let us not be unkind. I wish her well as – well, let's face it, she has given me the best gift she could. She has given me my freedom. I could not have moved with you to Athens had that not been so.'

'I do not know how people live in Athens with such high rents,' Thanasis says. 'If it was not for Papous renting out his taverna and coming to Athens so I could live with him I could not have survived on the wage I was paid.' He looks first at Juliet and then Mitsos.

'I always thought renting here in Greece was cheap,' Juliet interjects.

'Depends on your wage, and where you live.' Thanasis shrugs and Vasso pours Juliet some more wine. 'But will someone please tell me what is going on?'

'Okay.' Vasso taps her glass with her fork to get everyone's attention. 'So, Stamatis increased the rent on his taverna and the lease on the taverna Spiros and I had in Saros has come up for renewal. So...'

'So Vasso phoned me,' Stamatis takes over. 'And made the suggestion–'

'–that they come down here and open a taverna together!' Vasso finishes with triumph.

Thanasis looks from Vasso to Stamatis as this news sinks in. Grinning, he throws his head back, arms in the air, and looking up at the sky he mutters words of thanks to the stars. With one arm dropping behind Stamatis and one behind Vasso he rocks forward and pulls them both towards him in one huge embrace. 'Is it true?' he asks, his joy evident. 'Is it? Shall we all be together?'

'Yes.' Vasso's eyes shine as she looks into his face. 'We can be together, and you will both have work.'

'And Stamatis will live with us?'

'Of course!'

'Oh, this is wonderful,' Juliet adds.

'This is how it should be,' Stella informs anyone who cares to listen.

'Bravo!' Mitsos raises his glass to Stamatis, Stamatis lifts his in return, and then everyone is lifting theirs too.

'*Yamas!*' they cry into the stillness of the village, and somewhere high in the hills a dog answers.

Vasso looks up into the night sky, at the stars that appear endless and without number. As she stares, she notices one that is moving, glinting in the bright moonlight. Perhaps it's an aeroplane. As she watches, she wonders what it must be like, travelling so high and at such a great speed; and as she ponders this, she decides that life moves fast enough with her feet on the ground, and the truth is that she has no wish to go anywhere.

If you enjoyed The Rush Cutter's Legacy please share it with a friend, and check out the other books in the Greek Village Collection!

I'm always delighted to receive email from readers, and I welcome new friends on Facebook.

https://www.facebook.com/authorsaraalexi
saraalexi@me.com

Happy reading,

Sara Alexi